"Darren W. ... people in the world, only about ten percent have our abilities. You should be very proud of what you can do. I'll let you in on a little secret. Being a magician is a wonderful thing. Some magicians seek fame and rock star status and flaunt their abilities in front of the world while remaining cleverly disguised. Other magicians prefer to avoid the attention and to conform to what the world believes magicians to be— illusionists who use apparatus to demonstrate what they can do. Skeptics will always try to disprove the magic, but that's okay. This ensures people will never discover what we really are—true magic, of course!"

A huge smile lit up Vanrick's face as he gestured Darren to come forward. Together, they climbed the two steps onto the platform.

Note for Librarians: A cataloguing record for this book is available from Library and Archives Canada at www.collectionscanada.ca/amicus/index-e.html
ISBN 1-4120-8991-3

Printed in Victoria, BC, Canada. Printed on paper with minimum 30% recycled fibre.
Trafford's print shop runs on "green energy" from solar, wind and other environmentally-friendly power sources.

TRAFFORD
PUBLISHING™
Offices in Canada, USA, Ireland and UK

Book sales for North America and international:
Trafford Publishing, 6E–2333 Government St.,
Victoria, BC V8T 4P4 CANADA
phone 250 383 6864 (toll-free 1 888 232 4444)
fax 250 383 6804; email to orders@trafford.com
Book sales in Europe:
Trafford Publishing (UK) Limited, 9 Park End Street, 2nd Floor
Oxford, UK OX1 1HH UNITED KINGDOM
phone 44 (0)1865 722 113 (local rate 0845 230 9601)
facsimile 44 (0)1865 722 868; info.uk@trafford.com
Order online at:
trafford.com/06-0747

10 9 8 7 6 5 4 3 2

DISAPPEARANCE:

The First Part of Trickery and Honest Deception

For my husband, Jason, my best friend and inspiration
Thank you, as always,
for your keen eye, encouragement and support
To my son, Hayden, may you always
love books the way you do right now,
even though you aren't yet old enough to read them
For the young and the young at heart, may you always
believe in magic.

DISAPPEARANCE:

The First Part of Trickery and Honest Deception

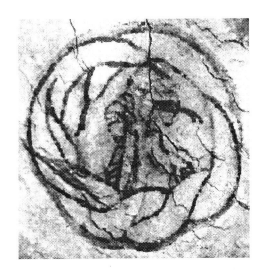

Rachelle G. Adamchuk

Chapter One

-Secret-

Dis-ap-pear-ance: To cease to be seen; vanish. To cease existing. The act of leaving secretly or without explanation. The event of passing out of sight. Gradually ceasing to be visible. (Webster's New World Dictionary)

It was dark; there was no doubt about that. He continued to walk forward down the long narrow corridor toward the light and what could only be the end of the journey. As he walked, he could hear the faint sound of laughter and music but couldn't make out what was going on. He was drawn to the light and the sound. The corridor seemed to go on forever as he hurried to reach the end. Suddenly, his path was eclipsed by a shadow, the black figure of a man standing in the light.

"We've been expecting you for quite some time now. You are later than we had anticipated," the shadow told him.

"What am I late for? What is this place?" he asked, quickening his pace towards the man in the light.

"In good time, Darius. In good time—"

The shadow paused as the walls along the dark corridor began to shift and buckle.

"No, wait! My name isn't Darius."

He stopped for a moment to try and grasp what was happening. The corridor was shaking and rumbling as the walls rippled and twisted. Huge beams of bright light shone through the widening fissures in the walls. He heard a loud explosion and the corridor blew apart, scattering debris everywhere. Momentarily blinded by the blast, he rubbed his burning eyes. His face stung, as the vicious wind pelted him with bits of plaster and wood. Shielding his face with his arms, he strained to see the figure that had been standing before him only seconds before. The man had disappeared.

The light at the end of the corridor was quickly advancing towards him as the wind continued to tear the place apart. He was overcome by fear. A strange sense of foreboding came over him.

Without warning, the white light exploded and sent him flying backwards through the air. The noise was deafening...

Darren Whalley sat up in one swift motion, his dark hair disheveled from another night of troubled sleep. For the past few weeks, he had been having a string of bizarre dreams. They had started one night, out of the blue. The dreams were quite different from his usual dreams; they were darker and more disturbing. In these dreams, he was

2

running towards or away from something. He sensed the dreams were significant and that time was somehow involved. Running out of time. Not enough time...it was confusing. The first dreams had been particularly puzzling, with their short bursts of images and nothing that made much sense. In some of these, he dreamed he was flying, something he hadn't dreamed about since he was a little boy. He would fly over his town and other places he had never been before. Sometimes he would see shadowy outlines of faces of people he had never met. He saw explosions, water, rocks, dirt, sand, candles, skulls, clowns and Ferris wheels, and heard snippets of conversations but couldn't make out what was being said. He had no idea what it all meant.

Darren had always thought of himself as just an average guy who never really had to struggle for anything. He wasn't the most popular kid in school, but was well known and liked. His best friend was like a brother to him. Of course, he would never tell him that! He had gone on a couple of dates with the most beautiful girl in the school, which made him the envy of all his friends. He got good grades and was good at sports without really trying. He enjoyed working out at the local gym, jogging and being part of the wrestling team.

Darren rubbed his eyes and looked around his bedroom. It looked like a normal, sixteen-year-old boy's room—tidier and more sparsely furnished than his sister Sarah's room. Darren and his sister Sarah were best friends. In fact if they weren't just over a year apart in age, one might think they were twins. Darren had always been protective of his little sister. At sixteen, he was very much the "big brother" and felt it was his duty to make sure that no harm came to her.

At fifteen, Sarah was very mature and felt very responsible for her brother and the rest of her family. She was very attractive with dark brown hair and an athletic build. When her daring nature landed her in trouble (which it often did!), her quick thinking usually bailed her out. She was brave and strong, qualities Darren admired. Like the time when they were riding their bicycles on the trails in the forest behind their house. Sarah had chosen an overgrown, rundown path. Her bicycle had veered off the trail and traveled over loose rock, dirt, pine needles, and branches, vibrating uncontrollably. Sarah had to think quickly before the bike threw her off into the thick, forested ravine. She jerked the handlebar to correct the bike, but the overcorrection caused the front tire to hit a branch in mid-turn. The tire twisted sideways and Sarah lost control of the bike and flew head first over the handlebar. Luckily, she was wearing her helmet, but she wasn't wearing knee or elbow pads.

Darren's heart had stopped beating and all the air in his lungs disappeared as he watched in horror as she crumpled to the ground. He jumped off his bike and let it fall with a clatter to the ground. He ran to Sarah, who was sitting on the dirt trail holding her hands out in front of her. When he squatted down next to her, he saw that her palms were scratched and bloody and one of her knees was

4

scraped raw and full of little pebbles. Darren felt horrible, like it had been entirely his fault. As he gently removed the tiny rocks and debris from Sarah's palms, he apologized for taking her to those trails and not to the new paved ones in the park. With tears welling up in her eyes, Sarah had smiled and said, "Don't worry, big brother. I like these trails. They're more fun than the other ones and just full of surprises. I'll heal up just fine, you'll see. It's just a flesh wound after all." Darren had chuckled at that, proud of his little sister.

Darren threw back the covers and swung off the bed, landing with a thud, face down on the bedroom floor.

"Damn it!" he cursed as he slowly pushed himself up off the floor.

He glanced over his shoulder at his bed which, sure enough, was floating about two feet off the floor. This had been a common occurrence the past few mornings, and it made no more sense to him now than it did the first time it happened. He knew he should have been careful getting out of bed, but had secretly hoped things had finally returned to normal. The first morning this had happened, the bed had floated and vibrated uncontrollably. He hadn't got up until the bed had gently returned to the floor by itself. The same thing had happened the following morning, but this morning was different.

As Darren sprang to his feet, he was startled by a loud crash behind him. He turned around to see that the bed had finally settled on the floor.

"What in the world—" he said with a startled look on his face.

"What was that?" asked Sarah, peering around Darren's bedroom door.

"Nothing. I just fell out of bed," Darren replied with an awkward smile.

"Little old to be falling out of bed, don't you think?" she asked, raising her eyebrows.

"Yeah, I guess so," he answered, pulling a T-shirt over his head.

"Hey, what's going on up there?" Mr. Whalley shouted as he climbed the stairs to Darren's room at the top of the stairs. "It sounded like an elephant just fell on the roof!"

Mr. Whalley, a retired football player, was a large and rather intimidating man. He had retired from football because of severe knee injuries. Despite several attempts at corrective surgery, his knee never worked as well as it did before. An exceptional father and a loving husband, he loved nothing more than spending time with his family. He enjoyed taking Sarah and Darren camping, fishing and to baseball games. The most memorable experience he has had with his children was at a baseball game several years earlier. His favorite team was playing and the batter was up. The batter struck the ball so hard it catapulted into the stands. Mr. Whalley hoisted Darren up into the air and extended his little gloved hand. To everyone's surprise, he caught the baseball! Even though Mr. Whalley knew that catching that ball must have stung his hand something awful, Darren never let him know it. He was so proud of his little boy.

Mr. Whalley also ran the family business, *Whalley's Treasures and Peculiar Treats*, which specialized in antiques and rare artifacts. The business often took him on the road in his quest for unique finds for the store. Although he enjoyed the travelling, it took him away from his family, often for weeks at a time.

"Oh, that was just Darren falling out of bed," offered Sarah.

"Hmm, thought you outgrew that years ago," Mr. Whalley replied with a smirk.

Sarah and their dad walked out of the bedroom and down the stairs.

"Yeah, so did I," Darren mumbled as he tried to tame the stubborn cowlicks in his hair.

He was agitated and a little frightened about the strange bed phenomenon and the bizarre dreams. Why would his bed be floating? He didn't know who to talk to about this, or if he even should. If he confided in someone about the bed, would that person think he was crazy? This whole thing was entirely too much to handle right now with finals on his mind. How on earth was he supposed to wrap his brain around exams in this last week of school when all he could think about was a bed that seemed to have a mind of its own!

Breakfast was the usual bowl of cereal eaten in a hurry. That morning, Darren chose to stand at the kitchen counter so he could eat it quickly and then dash.

"Can I catch a ride with you this morning?" Sarah asked, gobbling down a cereal bar.

"Sure. What exam do you have today?"

"English. I can't wait for summer break!"

"Yeah, me too," Darren agreed, putting his empty cereal bowl in the kitchen sink.

Mrs. Whalley entered the kitchen and grabbed a cereal bar to stuff in her purse. "Are you two still here? Aren't you going to be late?" she asked, pouring herself a glass of orange juice. She was tall and lean, and her long, dark hair was pulled back in a youthful ponytail.

Mrs. Whalley, one of the town's doctors, specialized in Pediatrics. A naturally generous and loving person, she adored working with children, and children loved her. But she was a wife and mother first; her son and daughter were her pride and joy. Her heart broke every time they came home with a bump, bruise, cut or scrape. Being a doctor didn't make it any easier to deal with her own children's pain and discomfort. She couldn't bear the thought of something horrible happening to them.

"We were just leaving. Are you ready to go, Sarah?" asked Darren.

"You bet! Let's fly!" Sarah pocketed another cereal bar, gave her mom a hug and headed out the door.

"See you after school, Mom," Darren said as he followed his sister out the door.

The drive to school was pleasant. The sun was shining, and many people were out walking their dogs or making their way to work or school. Darren loved his town—

although it could hardly be called a town anymore since it had been growing steadily every year. It was full of people who had traded the hustle and bustle of the big city for a quiet suburban lifestyle in a place where people were friendly and didn't hesitate to help out in times of need. Luckily, it wasn't yet large enough to suffer from any of the "big city" maladies that plagued some of the more cosmopolitan centres. To him, it was just the right size, the perfect place for kids to grow up.

Carlton Senior High wasn't a large school but it was big enough to comfortably accommodate all the young people in grades eight through twelve. The students were from all walks of life. The kids from wealthy families got along just fine with the ones from poor families. Occasionally, a fight would break out, but no one worried about bullies because the community wouldn't stand for it.

Unlike many of the students who attended Carlton Senior High, Darren had many pleasant memories from his time there. One year, he struggled in art class and wasn't able to come up with a project to submit to the teacher. He needed to do well on the project in order to boost the final grade on his first-term report card. After mulling it over for days, an idea finally came to him. He would paint a sepia-tone painting of an airplane! Using burnt umber and white oil-based paint on canvas, he created a pretty good likeness of an old plane in flight. With butterflies in his stomach and a lump in his throat, he submitted the painting to his teacher. To his surprise, she was so pleased with his work that she hung the painting in the main hallway of the school, where it remained for the rest of the school year! He received an "A" for his efforts and gained a new, deeper appreciation for art as well as a sense of pride in his newfound talent.

When Sarah and Darren arrived at school, they noticed a group of students had gathered in the parking lot. As they approached, Darren's best friend Joe Logan ran over to them from the center of the group.

"Have you heard?" Joe asked with urgency in his voice. "It's terrible! I just can't believe it!"

"Can't believe what? What are you talking about?" Darren asked, staring at Joe.

"It's Jessica. You know, Jessica Libben. She's been taken! Kidnapped! She's just disappeared! They think it happened last night right after she left the bowling alley."

"Oh, my goodness! That's terrible!" Sarah exclaimed, holding her hand over her mouth. "She's only two years older than me. How horrible! Her family must be going crazy!"

"Not only her family. Try the entire town! I thought you would have heard about this already," Joe said, looking over at the group of students.

He sat down on a bench next to the school's entrance. "Do the police have any leads? Do they know anything?"

"Not a thing. It's just so weird. Nothing like this has ever happened in our town before. Well, not that I know of anyway," Joe said, sitting next to Darren on the bench.

"Joe, I know this doesn't sound very good, but in light of what's happened, have we heard anything about exams today? Are they still on?" Sarah asked sheepishly.

"No one's informed us that we could bail out of school today. It's a shame, really. It would be nice, under the circumstances."

"No, I imagine the teachers want to get summer break under way as much as we do," Darren said, lowering his head and staring at his hands. "I'm sure they'd like it to begin sooner rather than later, in spite of what's happened. I sure hope Jessica's alright."

A kidnapping! It was very rare to have such things occur in their small town. He didn't want to imagine what could have happened to Jessica. He had gone to the movies a few times with her this past school term, and had really liked her. She was a very nice person, and well liked. It didn't make sense that someone would kidnap her. It made even less sense that she would run away; she just wasn't that type of person. *What a strange world we live in,* he thought.

Darren stared at Sarah and Joe as they continued chatting. Joe Logan was their best friend, and the three of them had grown up together. Joe was a few inches taller than Darren and had his mother's blonde hair. Although Joe could be a hothead at times, he was also a free spirit and very spontaneous. He had to work hard to get Darren to relax and take chances. On the other hand, Darren had to work hard to get Joe to slow down, think things through and take things more seriously.

Darren and Joe both had treasured memories of lazy, hot summers spent swimming in the lake (the local kids called it Marble Lake because its real name, Marabelliantian Lake, was just too difficult to pronounce), running, climbing, jumping, bike riding and ball playing, which invariably resulted in cuts and bruises, dirty hands, dirty feet and faces, torn clothes, stained runners and broken bones. Occasionally, Darren still felt pain behind his left eye where Joe had planted a baseball during one of their idle afternoons playing catch with Mr. Whalley in the backyard. Joe still had the two-inch scar on his back from a fall he had taken when he and Darren had been hiding out in their secret hideaway.

Their hideout was an old, abandoned house scheduled for demolition. The boarded-up windows and doors had been too tempting for them—or rather, Joe—to ignore. With a little coaxing, he convinced Darren to help peel back one of the boards from a broken window. They climbed into the house to investigate and pretended that ghosts roamed the empty rooms and hallways. The spooky, deserted old house was the best secret hideout a kid could ask for, and they had it all to themselves! Darren's sister was the only other person who knew about it.

During one of their afternoons in their hideout, Joe climbed up the stairs to the second floor, which they both did a hundred times during their countless visits to the house. One of the uncarpeted, wooden steps about halfway up was loose and when Joe stepped on the edge of the step it flipped up in the air like a skateboard. Joe lost his footing and tumbled to the bottom of the stairs. He lay in a crumpled heap, moaning and nearly unconscious. He was banged up pretty bad and bleeding. Terrified, Darren helped Joe to his feet, propped him up against his ten-year-old body and half carried, half dragged his friend to help.

Their secret hideout wasn't a secret anymore. Joe got fifteen stitches and a tongue-lashing from his parents. Darren received a lecture about how dangerous it was to horse around in a condemned house, especially without anyone's knowledge. Darren was also commended for his quick thinking and keeping his wits about him in a time of crisis. The house was eventually demolished, and that was the end of their hideaway.

Joe's mother, who worked as a lab technician at *Saint Margaret's Memorial Hospital*, was Mrs. Whalley's long-time friend. Joe's father owned *Logan's Flight Center*, a small airport just outside of town, where people learned to fly small two- and four-seater planes. Joe's dad flew people from their town to other nearby towns and cities. Joe was thrilled because his dad had finally agreed to teach him how to pilot a plane. This was all a little freaky to Darren, who preferred to keep his feet firmly planted on the ground, or at least let someone else pilot the darn plane. It would be a long time before he'd climb into a plane piloted by Joe. Perhaps it would be a different story after Joe actually got his license.

"Well, guys, I'm gonna get going," said Sarah. "I'll see you two later." She ran up the stairs, walked through the front door and disappeared in the crowd of people in the hallway.

The big gathering in the school parking lot was breaking up and the students were heading to their classes. Darren and Joe followed the crowd into the school.

Chapter Two

-Freak-

"One, two, three—"

Pinned on the mat, Darren felt lightheaded. He was sure he had pinched a nerve or something and would pass out if he didn't react quickly. Lifting his shoulders off the mat, he thrust his body upwards and knocked Scott Firth onto his back. Darren quickly spun around and landed on top of Scott, locking one arm around his neck and the other around his leg. The count started again and then stopped. Darren had succeeded in pinning Scott.

The gym erupted in cheers and hoots. Darren was pretty pleased with himself as he stood up and smiled down at Scott. Darren held out his hand to help Scott up, but Scott swatted his hand as he jumped to his feet, glaring at Darren.

"Get outta my face!" he shouted, shoving Darren out of his way.

Scott stalked over to the bench where the rest of the team was sitting and grabbed his towel. Unaware that Joe was sitting on part of the towel, he quickly turned around and stormed off to the locker room. When the towel remained pinned on the bench under Joe's firmly planted read end, Scott spun around and lost his footing. To add insult to his injured pride, he also slipped on some spilled water, lost his balance and fell to the gymnasium floor.

Bewildered, Joe stood up and looked down at Scott. "Oh, man, I'm really sorry. I didn't realize I was sitting on your towel!" he said innocently.

"I'm going to rip your bloody head off!" bellowed Scott as he got up from the floor and lunged at Joe. Darren ran towards them and caught Scott in mid-leap.

"Darren, get outta my way!" Scott hollered at Darren as he struggled to reach Joe. "I'm going to rip your girlfriend's head off and then I'm going to kick your ass!"

"What the hell is your problem, Scott? Just settle down!" yelled Darren.

A small crowd had gathered around them, and people were cheering them on in the hopes of seeing a fight. Scott broke free of Darren's grip and lunged at Joe, punching him square in the nose. He stopped suddenly and turned to look at Darren, anticipating that he might attack him from behind. Instead, Darren pushed past him to get to Joe. Scott seized the opportunity to walk to the locker room.

"Crap, Darren, I think he broke it!" moaned Joe, sitting back down on the bench with his head tilted back and pinching his nose.

"Let me look at it," Darren said, moving closer. "It's not broken. You're lucky he can't throw a punch. I think Sarah could punch harder than him."

Joe quickly got back up to his feet, but Darren grabbed him by the arm.

"Darren let me at him! It's not right! I'm sick of his bull! Who does he think he is, anyhow?! Freakin' 'roid monkey! And where the hell is coach Marrows?" Joe barked, looking around the gymnasium.

"It's not worth it, Joe. Scott's a jerk and we all know it. He's pissed because he was off his game this match. We only have a few more days before we're out of here, so don't do anything stupid," warned Darren in his usual calm and collected manner.

"He didn't seem off his match to me. Looked to me like you were getting your butt kicked," Joe said with a smirk as he tried to stand up. He quickly sat back down again, looking a little shaky. "On second thought, I think I'll sit for a bit."

"Yeah, who was getting his butt kicked?" Darren teased. "Well, I'm going to shower," he said as he headed for the locker room.

Since the fight hadn't materialized, the crowd dispersed. As usual, Darren was amazed at how quickly people congregated to watch something that was none of their business.

The locker room was empty as he made his way to the locker where he had put his belongings. His mind was reeling from the events of the day so far. He thought about Jessica and immediately felt sad and helpless. He remembered when they had gone to the movie just over a month ago. When they left the theater, they had decided to go for a walk. They had sat in the nearby park and laughed at each other's stories about growing older and all the crazy things they had done as kids.

He was standing directly in front of his locker in deep thought when a sudden force jarred him out of his reverie, sending him head first into the locker door. He spun around and put his hands around his attacker's neck to prevent being struck again. He was surprised to see Scott facing him.

"Scott, lay off, will you! It's over, for crying out loud!" Darren hollered. He could feel Scott relax somewhat. "If I let you go, will you calm down?"

"Yeah, just let go!" Scott yelled at Darren.

Darren couldn't understand why Scott was so angry. He hesitated for a few seconds before releasing his grip on him. "What's gotten into you?"

"You cheated! I had you pinned!" Scott exclaimed.

"If you had me pinned correctly, I wouldn't have been able to slip out of the hold and pin you so easily," Darren explained. "Don't you think this is rather juvenile? I mean, come on, we've known each other a long time and have been on the same wrestling team for years."

"Sure, and it's about time someone taught you a lesson," Scott bellowed. Without warning, he lunged at Darren, knocking him to the floor. Then he jumped on top of him and straddled his chest. "It's your fault!" he shouted angrily, grabbing him by the throat.

"What's my fault? I don't understand. Scott, what is this *really* about?" Darren asked, sprawled out on the floor with Scoot looming over him.

"Jess!" he whined. "I don't understand where Jess has gone! If you'd just left us alone, she'd still be here," Scott said, loosening his grip.

"Oh, come on! I didn't have anything to do with what's happened to Jessica. I never got between you two. I stopped seeing her when she started going out with you," Darren argued, trying to shove Scott off him.

"I don't believe you! I've seen the way she looks at you!" Scott yelled. He began to choke Darren again. Darren was beginning to feel light headed. He was blacking out. He was really going to pass out this time. He needed to do something right away. There was no time to lose. He tried lifting his legs to form a bridge in an attempt to buck Scott off. It didn't work. Darren started to panic. He couldn't breathe. Scott's grip loosened slightly around his throat.

Darren lifted his right arm and extended his palm in a pleading gesture. "Get off me!" he screamed.

Suddenly, Darren no longer felt the weight of Scott's body. No more choking. No more pain or dizziness.

Scott felt himself being lifted into the air and hurled across the room. He smashed into the lockers on the opposite wall with such force that they dented inward. Scott slumped to the floor. It took him a few minutes to figure out that he was no longer trying to choke someone. "What the hell did you do?" he asked incredulously as he stood up, favoring his left side.

Darren sat up in shock. He had no idea what had just happened. How had he thrown a person across a room without even touching him?

"You're a *freak*! A bloody freak!" Scott yelled, fear clearly registering on his face and in his voice.

"Scott, I can explain—" Darren started to say as he approached Scott. In truth, however, he was terrified. How could he explain what had just happened when he didn't understand it himself!

"Stay away from me! My God, what *are* you? Just stay away from me! I mean it!" Scott turned and ran from the locker room, holding his left arm against his body.

Darren was alone in the locker room. This was officially the weirdest day he had ever experienced. *Something very strange is happening,* Darren thought as he finished his shower, got dressed and headed out of the gymnasium. He was walking down the hall when he caught up with Sarah, who looked at him with a puzzled expression on her face.

"Scott's saying some pretty weird things about you. He's calling you a freak or something," she said, putting an arm around his shoulder. All the students stared at them in the hall as they passed by.

"What kind of crap is he making up this time?" Darren asked, looking straight ahead at the exit doors in front of them.

"Well," she said teasingly. "He isn't saying anything new. I've always known you were a freak."

Darren stopped walking and stared at her, trying to read her eyes. He was scared. Did she know about the weird stuff that had been happening to him? Had she seen him floating in bed? He shook his head in an attempt to dismiss these thoughts from his mind. "You know me, sis. I'm as freaky as they get."

"Yeah? If you want to talk freaky, let's talk about Joe," she said, giggling.

"He can be pretty weird, all right, but that's what we like about him. I can honestly say I'm glad Scott's graduating this year and won't be around for my grade twelve year," Darren added with a chuckle, relieved that the conversation had drifted away from what had happened in the locker room. He was still confused. What had been going on these past few days? Nothing made sense. As if being a teenager wasn't enough of a struggle, now he had something new to deal with and hide in order to fit in. It just wasn't fair. His mind was reeling as he walked to his car with Sarah.

The drive home was pleasant. The Whalleys lived in a nice area with lots of trees and friendly neighbors. The park that he and Sarah visited many times over the years was only a few blocks away. The little coffee shop where Darren enjoyed the occasional iced Frappuccino was at the end of their street. As he neared the house, he could see Joe in the front yard wrestling with Bruce, the Whalley family's golden retriever.

"Hey, Spaz, you beat us here!" Sarah exclaimed.

"Yup. Had to stop by for a romp with my pal Brucey," Joe said, grabbing Bruce playfully by the scruff of the neck and pinning him in a choke hold. Bruce wriggled and bucked before breaking free and tackling Joe, licking his face continuously.

"Hey, traitor, you're supposed to be my wrestling partner," Darren said, walking over to Bruce and Joe. Crouching down, he wrapped his arms around Bruce's ribcage and gave him a hug. "Are ya hungry, big fella?"

"Yeah, I actually am a bit peckish, thanks," replied Joe, walking up the stairs to the house. Sarah had made her way inside the house while the guys were horsing around with the dog.

"You do know I was talking to Bruce, right?" Darren laughed at his friend.

"Of course," Joe said smugly as he opened the front door. "Age before beauty," he said, bowing.

"Hmm, you like playing up this one-month-older-than-you thing, don't you?" Darren smiled at him.

"Well, sure. Why not?" Joe replied as he opened the refrigerator and grabbed a can of pop. "I heard there was some commotion in the locker room after the gym cleared out today. Scott ran outta the gym, just flipping out. It was hilarious. I would love to have seen what you did. He was as white as a ghost and saying some crazy stuff about you being a freak of nature or something."

"What crazy stuff was he saying?" Darren asked nervously.

"Well, that's the thing. He didn't really say. He just kept going on about your being a strange freak or whatever and that what you did was impossible. But who really listens to him anyway? He's just a big knuckle dragger," Joe sat down at the kitchen table. "So what really did happen?"

"Nothing that incredible," Darren replied and proceeded to describe the incident—minus the part when he threw Scott across the room without actually touching him. "Then I just punched him in the arm and pushed with all my might until he flew backwards. The end. Nothing more to it." Despite his best efforts, Darren wondered if he had been less than convincing.

Joe nodded. "Well, I can see where he came up with such an elaborate story. For some bizarre reason, he was trying to make himself out to be a total wimp and a loon, and he succeeded. So, what's for dinner?"

"Aren't your parents expecting you for dinner?" Darren asked. He had pulled out a chair and was sitting across from Joe at the kitchen table, sipping his pop.

"Probably. Hey, the Carnival is coming to town next week! We're going, right? It should be fun."

"That's right. I had completely forgotten about it," Darren replied. A smile formed on his lips and he added, "Do you remember last year when we made that bet? Whoever stayed on the Zipper for the most rides would win the grab bag. I lucked out and got my one and only hockey card—the limited edition Chuck Everson hockey card that you so desperately wanted—and your first edition Knights Crossing comic book."

"I remember." Joe smiled weakly. He shifted in his seat and took another sip of pop.

"I sure did enjoy that comic."

"You'd better still be enjoying it! Do you know how much it's worth? Oh well, giving it to you was worth it. I enjoyed watching you turn green and throw up all over the place," Joe said, laughing at the memory.

"Let's not do that again this year, okay?" Darren made a sour face and held his stomach.

Mr. Whalley walked in the door carrying a bag of groceries. "How does spaghetti sound for dinner?" he asked, putting the bag down on the counter and pulling out a jar of pasta sauce.

"Sounds delicious," Joe and Darren replied in unison.

"Spaghetti it is then. Where's Sarah?"

"She went up to her room. She needed some girl time," Darren intoned, rolling his eyes.

"Say, son, you're going to help me out with the store again this summer, right? I'd hate to break our tradition. Besides, you seem to have a knack for antiques," he added.

"Yeah, sure, I'll help out. Still part time, right? Maybe when I graduate from high school next year, I could put in more time. Right now I just want to enjoy summer break as much as I can."

"That should work out just fine," Mr. Whalley said with a smile.

Chapter Three

-Sleight of Hand-

School was finally over for the season and summer was under way. Darren continued to experience the strange bed phenomenon and had figured out that if he acknowledged what was happening when the bed was floating, he could also make the bed land on the floor gently by just thinking about it. If only he could figure out how to prevent it from rising in the first place! He was determined to understand what was happening to him.

Jessica was still missing. It had been over a week and the police still didn't have much to go on. Jessica's family appeared on the news, pleading for the return of their daughter. They also put up "missing" posters in the local shops in the hopes that someone might have some information. Jessica's picture was everywhere, showing off her beautiful, smiling face, her blonde hair in the cute pixie cut and her sparkling blue eyes so full of life. The people Darren knew in his community were still talking about the kidnapping. Understandably, they were all concerned that it might happen to their own kids. Some people had already decided that Jessica would never return and were speculating about the horrible things that could have happened to her. Darren couldn't bear to hear them talk about her that way. Rather than risk losing his temper (or throwing someone without actually laying a finger on them), he found it best to quickly leave the vicinity of their discussions.

As soon as school ended for the year, Darren began working for his dad at *Whalley's Treasures and Peculiar Treats*. One day when he was alone, he saw Scott Firth outside the store. As usual, he wore his naturally curly hair quite long, as was the style for soccer players. He was quite good at soccer—much better than he was at wrestling. If Scott aspired to be a professional soccer player, his chances were pretty good, as scouts were always checking out their school soccer games. The husky seventeen-year-old, Scott was usually confident and outgoing—a typical jock. But on this day, he looked somber and was walking with his head hung low and his shoulders slumped.

Darren would like to have spoken to him about Jessica and let him know he shouldn't give up hope, but the last thing he wanted was another confrontation. As it turned out, though, he never got the opportunity. When Scott saw him through the store window, his expression changed to surprise (or was it fear?) He immediately averted his gaze and walked briskly across the street.

Just as Scott disappeared, Darren saw Sarah and Joe walking down the sidewalk towards the shop—Sarah carrying a cup in each hand, and Joe holding a cup in one hand while eagerly devouring the sandwich he held in the other. They walked into the store and approached Darren.

"I got you a Frapp," Sarah said, handing it to him. She sat down on a stool next to the counter.

"Thanks, I could use one. It's been slow today. Not as many tourists. I guess everyone is at the Carnival." Darren took a sip of his Frappuccino.

"Do you want to go to the Carnival after you close up tonight?" Joe enquired as he walked around sipping his drink and checking out sundry items on the shelves.

The store was small but clean and tidy, unlike the state it was in when Mr. Whalley had bought it. The store had been around for many years and had been dusty, cluttered and unkempt. People walking out of the store would feel dirty and itchy, like they needed a shower, or at the very least, like they had to wash their hands. It had taken a lot of work to make it look classy, warm and welcoming. The town had lots of tourists, so business was always good. And since Darren's father travelled far and wide to collect antiques and collectibles, people from all over the world would bring things to him or come in to buy. Darren liked working in the shop; it was fun meeting so many different people and learning about other parts of the world.

"I'll be closing up in an hour and then I'll definitely be ready for the Carnival," Darren answered.

Joe made his way up the flight of stairs to the antique books and smaller antique collectibles. "Hey, what's this supposed to be?" he asked, holding up a silver wand with a small bowl at the end.

"It's a cigar snuffer," Sarah piped up.

"Yeah, okay. That's *weird.*" Joe grimaced as he put it back on the shelf. "People sure do collect the strangest stuff."

"You're insane," teased Sarah, giggling at his facial expression.

"That particular snuffer is from 1730. Very rare," Darren stated.

"Hmmm," Joe muttered, feigning interest as he glanced at the other articles in the display case.

"Did Dad bring this back from Rome?" Sarah asked, holding up a necklace from the display case near the cash register. Before Darren could respond, she put the necklace back in its place and began looking at the other articles in the display case.

"Yes, as well as those rings, bracelets and earrings. That particular necklace is about two thousand years old," Darren said, sitting down next to her at the counter.

"Wow! What if it belonged to royalty or something?"

"It's always a possibility," Darren replied with a shrug.

"Must be worth a fortune," Joe commented as he wandered around looking at the books on the shelves. "How does he afford to purchase them? You know, in order to sell them here?"

"Dad has investments. And, if need be, the bank doesn't mind investing in these antiques, as it always gets its initial investment back in a timely manner," informed Sarah. "We do a lot of business, thanks to our web page and our walk-in sales. The web page is great. People all over the world can easily make purchases from the comfort of their own homes and we ship the items to them. We're always replenishing our inventory, hence our father's trips."

"You gotta' spend money to make money," remarked Joe. He picked up a book, smelled it, wrinkled up his nose and placed it back on the shelf amongst the other old tomes.

"You've got that right!" Darren said, smiling.

With Sarah and Joe there to keep Darren company, the hour passed quickly. After locking up the store and calling home to inform Sarah and Darren's parents where they were going, the three of them headed off to the carnival. They looked forward to the carnival each year. It came to their town at the end of the school term every year.

As they approached the entrance to the Carnival, Darren noticed that the Carnival seemed to be bigger than previous years. It had the usual rides, games and food but seemed to have a few new shows. Or perhaps the shows had always been there but he had never noticed them before.

The theme this year was "illumination" and was supposed to be really spectacular. The town would have to wait until dusk to get the full effect of all the lights. Darren, Sarah and Joe walked around checking out the sights and sounds. A clown walking on stilts stood out amongst the adults and children. A girl ran screaming from the house of horrors. Her boyfriend ran after her, laughing and assuring her that everything was all right. The tantalizing aroma of burgers, hot dogs, cotton candy and delicious hot mini donuts wafted through the air. The brilliant colors in the awnings, carts, costumes, lights, balloons, and cotton candy bobbing throughout the crowd created a festive ambience.

As was their tradition each Carnival season, the three of them went for a spin on the big, colorful Ferris wheel. After purchasing tickets for a few other rides, they proceeded to the Ferris wheel. Dusk loomed over the horizon as they stood in the line-up, talking and taking in the sights and sounds. Screams and laugher erupted from the rides.

After their ride on the Ferris wheel, they walked around and checked out the vendors and games where players could win little trinkets and stuffed animals.

"Hey, Darren, you wanna go on the zipper?" Joe asked with a smile.

"No, I think I'll pass this year," Darren answered, chuckling.

"So you learned your lesson last year," Sarah said with a smirk on her face.

"Can honestly say I'm not in a hurry to do that again," Darren said, walking with his arms behind his back.

"I think we've really grown a lot over this past year. Matured. You know, grown older and wiser. Wouldn't you agree, Darren?" Joe asked straightening up. He imitated Darren by crossing his arms behind his back.

"Sure do. We're much more mature," Darren replied, furrowing his brow in an attempt to look serious. He watched as a young boy shot targets in an attempt to win a stuffed toy.

"You guys are idiots," Sarah scoffed, as she wandered off to Whack-A-Mole.

"Darren, check this out!" shouted Joe, who was standing with a crowd of people at one of the shows. He looked over his shoulder at Darren, excitement written all over his face. Darren thought he must have spotted a really cute girl or something. Sarah finished whacking moles, collected a purple stuffed bear and wandered over to where Joe was standing. Darren walked over and stood next to them.

In front of them was a simply decorated platform. A man stood on the platform with a deck of cards in his hands. Darren figured he must have just finished some sort of sleight of hand trick. Behind him hung a poster that read *Unbelievable Magic Performed by the Great Alexius.* The magician jumped down from the platform, approached a young girl in the crowd and asked her to select a card from the deck. After she had selected a card, he asked her to show it to the audience but not to him. The young girl held the card very tightly against her chest as she turned to face the audience. She held up the card then quickly concealed it again. The card was the three of spades. Alexius, the magician, asked her to hold out the card face down. When she did as she was told, the card suddenly burst into flames. She screamed and dropped the card, which quickly burned to ashes and settled on the ground. Alexius asked her to reach into the back pocket of her mother's jeans. She did so and held up the card, squealing with delight. It was the three of spades! The girl jumped up and down, beaming as she clutched the card to her chest.

"That was really cool," said Sarah, wide-eyed.

Joe smirked. "Well, obviously, when the girl's mother turned to face the audience with her daughter he put the card in her pocket."

"Maybe so, but how would he have known which card it was," Sarah countered.

"Obviously, some magic is involved, of course," said Joe hotly.

"Obviously," Sarah replied smugly, turning her nose up at him and rolling her eyes. She faced the magician again. He was young, perhaps in his mid-twenties. He had blonde hair and wore a T-shirt and jeans, not the typical attire for a magician.

Alexius jumped back up onto the platform and walked over to a small table. He picked up a piece of fabric that had been lying on the table and revealed a transparent wax statue of a bird. Alexius instructed the audience to watch the statue very closely. Once again, he hopped down into the crowd and this time handed Sarah a pencil and a small piece of paper. He asked her to write a name down on the paper and not reveal it to anyone. Sarah looked at Joe and Darren. Joe shrugged. Darren smiled at her, finding this oddly exciting. Magic had never really appealed to him before.

After Sarah had written a name on the slip of paper, Alexius instructed her to fold the paper up so it was really small and then toss it in the air. When she did this, it exploded into a little puff of smoke and then disintegrated. With his head bowed, Alexius jumped back onto the stage and stood next to the wax bird.

Suddenly, the audience erupted in loud applause. Darren craned his neck to see what had happened. Sarah pushed her way through the crowd, anxious to find out what all the fuss was about. Alexius invited her up onto the stage. After calmly walking over to the bird, she gasped and covered her mouth with her hand. She stared at the statue in awe. There, inside the transparent bird, was an unfolded, crumpled little piece of paper with the name "Darren" written on it.

"Is that the piece of paper with the name you wrote on it?" asked Alexius.

Darren and Joe had reached the edge of the stage. Darren couldn't believe what he was seeing. He figured the secret to the previous trick was the lady planted in the audience, but this had blown that theory right out of the water.

"How did you do that?" asked Sarah, as she stared at the bird.

"Magic!" Alexius whispered.

Sarah walked to the edge of the platform and hopped back down into the audience to stand with Darren and Joe. Once again, she stared up at her handwriting on the little piece of paper inside the wax bird. Then Alexius clapped his hands very loudly. The audience jumped from the sudden sound. Alexius waved his hand over the wax statue, and in front of the stunned crowd, the statue transformed into a real live bird that squawked and flew away. The audience came alive with cheers and applause. Darren watched in amazement while Joe stood staring with his mouth agape.

"Thank you, thank you," Alexius said. "And now we shall say goodnight with one final act. Please remain silent."

Alexius inched backwards to the poster behind him and spread his arms. He looked down at his feet, and then slowly raised his head. *It couldn't be*, Darren thought as he looked at Alexius' feet. Darren stumbled backwards and gawked in disbelief as the man levitated two feet off the platform. As incredulous as this was, it was oddly familiar. The hair on the back of his neck stood up and chills ran down his spine. Could he do that? Was the bed-floating— or levitating—a sign of what he, himself, could do?

"Nothing more than pulling a rabbit out of a hat," explained Joe with his brow furrowed. Nonetheless, he looked very puzzled.

"Whatever. You saw what we saw. It was pretty unbelievable, that's for sure," Sarah remarked, still taken aback from the shock of what they witnessed. "I just can't explain it. My mind can't grasp it or come up with a reasonable explanation."

"I guess that's why it's called magic," Joe offered.

"It was supernatural," Darren said quietly.

"Yeah, it was. He was also very cute," Sarah added with a smirk.

"I'm starving," Joe said, making his way to a hamburger stand. "Are you guys hungry? I'm buying," He sat down on a stool at the counter. As far as he was concerned, the subject of magic was now closed.

Darren, on the other hand, was very much intrigued.

"Yeah, I could eat," Sarah agreed.

"Me, too," said Darren casually. "I'm just going to find a washroom. Meet you back here in a bit."

Darren walked in the direction of the magician's show and the tent attached to the platform where Alexius had performed.

Chapter Four

-Revealed-

Darren was oblivious to the activity going on around him. His mind was reeling. The magic tricks he had witnessed were fantastic! How were they done? How had Alexius inserted Sarah's written piece of paper inside the wax bird and then made the statue come alive and fly away? Joe's explanation couldn't be far off—magic had always been about illusions, right? There was obviously a logical explanation for what he had seen, including the levitation. He felt oddly elated. He needed to understand. He just had to see for himself.

Before he knew it, he was standing in front of the platform. The area was now deserted. Darren stepped up onto the stage and walked to the table where the bird had flown away. He squatted down and looked under what appeared to be an ordinary table. Nothing. He stood up and slowly ran his hand over the surface of the table. Nothing remarkable about its surface, either. Darren walked around the back wall where the poster hung and ran his hand over the wall board. Still nothing unusual. He lifted the poster. All clear. The platform itself was intact with no hatch doors.

Darren walked to the steps leading to the tent adjacent to the stage. He stepped down the two steps, turned right and walked down the short, dark corridor to the entrance. Once inside the tent, he could see tables, chairs, trunks, costumes, poster boards with other magicians' names on them, a sofa and a few armchairs. A deck of cards lay on a table in the center of the tent. He glanced around to make sure he was completely alone. Standing beside the table, he stared at the deck of cards. He positioned his right hand, palm side down, a few inches above the deck of cards. His held his hand in this position for a few moments before moving it slowly to the right. As he did so, the cards spread out face down on the tabletop. Darren drew in a deep breath and looked down at the cards. They looked like fallen dominos, perfectly laid out. He reached out, selected a card and flipped it face-up onto the table—it was the king of hearts. After inspecting the card closely, he took a deep, shaky breath and gently ripped it into many pieces that floated onto the table.

Darren could feel the hair on the back of his neck stand up as he glanced furtively around the tent. He didn't want anyone to see what he would do next. Taking another deep breath, he held his right hand out in front of him, flexed his fingers and envisioned the card whole again. The card's tiny pieces began to come together on the table beneath his hovering hand. The ripped seams on the card glowed for a brief moment. What lay on the tabletop was a perfectly formed king of hearts that didn't even look as though it had just been torn to pieces.

Darren expelled his breath. He felt dizzy and nauseous. *What is wrong with me? What is this all about?* Looking up, he noticed a small chair folded against a trunk a couple feet away from him. He reached out his left hand to pull the chair closer to him so he could sit down. The chair rose and catapulted into his open hand. Darren jumped up and gazed at his hand. *Okay, this is way too weird!* His weak knees began to buckle beneath him as he fell back down onto the chair. Bewildered, Darren stood up and again stared at the chair in his hand.

"Please sit," said a voice over his shoulder.

Darren jumped. He dropped the chair and spun around to face the voice behind him.

"Please, do sit down. It isn't every day you find out that you are extraordinary. Or perhaps I should phrase it as you did—supernatural," said the man kindly. He smiled and raised an eyebrow at Darren.

The man was tall with dark hair and sprinkles of salt and pepper-colored gray through the sides. His hair was styled in a fashionable longer style that was nicely kept. He was dressed in black slacks and a blue button-down shirt. He had an aura about him. He stood with poise and confidence. His eyes revealed years of knowledge as though he had hundreds of years of memories hidden away there, but his face was that of a forty-five perhaps fifty-five year old man. He had a truly powerful presence.

"We've been expecting you for quite some time now," the man said, grabbing another chair and sitting across from Darren, who was still standing and gawking at the man. "You're later than we expected."

This time, Darren's knees did give way. His legs turned to rubber and he fell hard on his rear on the floor of the tent. He had heard those words over and over again each night in his dreams.

"What do you mean by *supernatural?* What do you mean you've been expecting me and that I'm late? What's this all about? What's *happening* to me?" Frustrated, Darren sat on the floor and stared up at the man sitting in the chair smiling down at him. "And who are you?" he added.

"My name is Vanrick Frulis. I'm a lot like you and have been for many years. I, too, possess special abilities. We are not alone, you and I. Others also possess these abilities, as you witnessed earlier this evening. In the world of magic, we do not need to hide what we are. You are welcome to join us, this family of magicians with whom I travel."

"And what exactly are we? I don't know about you, but I was a perfectly normal guy until this strangeness started happening," Darren retorted.

"You are different, special, advanced. And, yes, we are considered strange— unbelievable, unfathomable, perhaps even eerie. You are late because these abilities usually surface in early puberty. You are well past that now, and as you said, you have been living as a perfectly normal guy." He stopped and smiled, his posture perfectly relaxed as he spoke.

"There is nothing "perfectly normal" about the things I can do. I can't even grasp what I'm doing or why these things are happening to me," Darren replied, beginning to panic.

"I understand, and in good time you will understand, too. Let us talk now about our world. Please take a seat in a chair so you will be more comfortable while we talk." Vanrick motioned slowly with his left hand and a chair across the room glided through the air and landed on the floor next to Darren.

"You and I possess powers beyond what others can comprehend. We are considered supernatural because what we are able to do cannot be explained by the laws of nature or science. There are unseen forces within us. Each of us has our own unique gifts—some have more than others; some are more powerful than others. Where does this power come from, you may ask? Well, it comes from deep within us, to be sure. Not everyone can tap into this ability. As you are now aware, the ability chooses you; you do not choose it. It is your birthright. You are born the way you are. Don't get me wrong—some people develop certain abilities themselves through years of stimulating certain parts of their brains. But they will never be where you and I are naturally." Vanrick paused to look around the room. "We should finish up soon, as people are looking for you."

"Oh, no! Joe and Sarah," Darren exclaimed, sitting forward in the chair.

"I would love to meet with you again. I have much to teach you. You would benefit from meeting the others in the magic act, as you share the same abilities," he said. He rose from his chair and gestured for Darren to stand.

"I have a lot of questions," Darren admitted.

Vanrick put his hand on Darren's shoulder. "I may not have answers to all your questions, but I will try my best to mentor you, if you wish," Vanrick offered. "Just remember that there is nothing wrong with you. You are unique, but you are not the monster some might have you believe. There is a time and a place to reveal your gifts, but it is not out in the open for everyone to see. Not without a disguise."

"A disguise? What do you mean? Like Batman? I'm not sure what you mean? Look, Vanrick, I can honestly say that when I saw the show tonight I didn't feel so alone. And when I came back here to prove to myself that I was capable of doing those same types of tricks, I felt more alive than ever before."

"Darren Whalley, out of the six billion people in the world, only about ten percent have our abilities. You should be very proud of what you can do. I'll let you in on a little secret. Being a magician is a wonderful thing. Some magicians seek fame and rock star status and flaunt their abilities in front of the world while remaining cleverly disguised. Other magicians prefer to avoid the attention and to conform to what the world believes magicians to be—illusionists who use apparatus to demonstrate what they can do. Skeptics will always try to disprove the magic, but that's okay. This ensures people will never discover what we really are—true magic, of course!"

A huge smile lit up Vanrick's face as he gestured Darren to come forward. Together, they climbed the two steps onto the platform.

"You know my name," said Darren. Vanrick smiled and nodded. Darren smiled and looked down at his feet. *Some pretty incredible things had happened tonight,* he thought. "Thanks for taking the time to talk to me," he said, walking across the platform. "Well, I guess this is goodbye."

"Not at all. We are here for three more nights. I would be glad to speak with you every night that we are here. That is completely up to you, of course. We can continue our conversation another evening. Until then, I bid you goodnight." He waved at Darren, then turned around and disappeared.

Darren blinked at the spot where Vanrick Frulis had been standing only moments earlier. He smiled to himself as he walked to the edge of the platform.

"Where have you been?" Sarah asked impatiently. "We've been looking all over for you." She was standing with her hands on her hips.

"Let me guess... number two," Joe said, mesmerized by some attractive girls entering the house of mirrors.

"You're gross!" Sarah exclaimed as she stormed off towards the exit gate.

"Well, I guess that's enough fun for one night," Joe declared as she walked away.

"I can't leave you two alone for a second," Darren teased.

"Hey, you were longer than a second. Did you get lost or something?"

"Yeah, something," Darren replied as they walked towards the House of Mirrors. He crammed his hands deep into his pockets. He felt really good. He hadn't felt this good since before Jessica went missing. The thought of Jessica brought on a momentary twinge of guilt. A great weight had been lifted off his shoulders. He finally had someone he could talk to about the strange things that were happening to him. He still had many questions, but he felt like he wasn't alone anymore and would be okay.

Darren was exhausted when they got home that evening. He climbed into bed and fell asleep instantly. He had a very vivid dream, and in his sleep he made up his mind. He knew what he had to do.

The next morning, Darren made his way down the hall to Sarah's bedroom. He stood outside her bedroom door for a couple of minutes contemplating what he would say to her. Last night, when he had made the decision to tell her, it seemed so much easier. Today, it didn't seem so easy. Darren's parents had both gone to work, so the coast was clear to talk without being overheard. Bruce had followed him up the stairs and stood staring at him.

"I know. I will. I just need a minute," Darren explained to Bruce as if the dog could read his mind. Darren raised his hand and knocked on the door. "Sarah, can I come in?" he asked through the door.

"Sure, what's up?" Sarah asked, as he opened the door and made his way across Sarah's very cluttered room. She collected books and posters of everything imaginable. Her laptop lay open on her messy desk. Sarah loved doing research. No doubt she had a plethora of useless information in her brain.

Darren walked over to the large comfy armchair by the window. "I thought school was over for the summer," he said, looking at all the papers and books on Sarah's desk.

"Mm-hmm. I was just looking into some things, that's all," she replied. She was lying down on the bed with a book in her lap.

"I see. What are you looking into?"

"Nothing interesting. Just stuff," she replied. She set the book aside before sitting up and crossing her legs. "What's going on? Why do you look more serious than usual?"

Darren leaned forward in the chair and rested his elbows on his knees. "I really need to tell you something, and it isn't easy," he said.

"Wow, this really sounds important," Sarah said, turning to face him.

"It is really important."

Darren proceeded to tell her about the levitating bed and what happened with Scott. He told her about the things he did in the magician's tent when he was supposedly in the washroom at the Carnival. Darren told her all about Vanrick Frulis and the insights he had shared with him regarding his abilities.

"I'm sorry, Darren, but this sounds like a really wonderful fantasy to me," Sarah announced when he was finished.

"I know. If I wasn't trying to come to terms with it myself, I would be thinking the same thing." He leaned forward in the chair and looked down at a book on the floor. "I'd like to show you something. I've been trying it out this morning. Don't freak out or anything."

He lifted his hand to knee level and let it hover over the book. The book lifted off the floor to a point midway to his hand. Then it began to slowly spin clockwise.

Sarah moved closer to the edge of the bed and swung her legs over the side. She braced herself with her arms stiff at her sides, holding herself steady. Darren let the book touch back down on the floor. "What else can you do?" she asked, her interest now peaked.

"I'm not entirely sure. I'm discovering new abilities all the time. Let's try something else," he said, holding his hand over the book again. This time he thought of one word: *vanish*. The book disappeared right before their eyes.

"Where did it go?" Sarah asked, incredulous.

Darren looked at the spot on the bed next to Sarah and held out his right hand in her direction. The book reappeared next to Sarah on the bed.

"I don't know where things go when they disappear, but I can always bring them back." He looked at Sarah's face. The wide-eyed expression on her face said it all.

"No wonder Scott thought you were a freak. Can't believe you scared the hell out of him. It isn't really that scary. I think it's really cool," she said excitedly.

"Well, I didn't throw you across the room," Darren said with a laugh. "You'd find that pretty freaky, I'm sure. I was pretty freaked out myself. Remember, I had never done anything like that before in my life."

"You must have been terrified. I've read about stuff like this. It isn't unheard of, you know. It's psychophysical phenomena, telekinesis, or perhaps a combination of both."

Darren could see that she was genuinely excited about his abilities. He was glad he had told her. She was trying to work it out in her own mind—sorting through the tidbits of related information she had stored in there.

"When are you going to tell Mom and Dad?" Sarah asked, looking up at Darren.

"I hadn't put much thought into that. I don't think I'll rush into it, though. Not everyone will be as open-minded as you are. Most people will think I'm a freak or that there's something wrong with me. I think I'll wait."

Darren didn't look forward to telling his parents. It wasn't easy talking to them about things like this. It would be the same as talking to them about his teenage changes or urges. It would just have to wait until he understood it better himself, until some questions were answered regarding how and why he had these abilities.

"They're our parents, Darren. They're not everyone. They'll understand. You have to give them a chance. You know they love you, and nothing you tell them will change that."

"You don't know that. You don't know how they'll react to having a son who isn't who they thought he was. We can't tell anyone, okay?" Darren pleaded, looking down at the floor again. He felt sad all of a sudden. The thought of not having his parents' support and love was hard to imagine, and it hurt him to think about it.

They finished their discussion and decided they were both feeling ravenous. They left the bedroom and went downstairs for some lunch

Chapter Five

-Mayday-

Darren and Sarah were just finishing up their lunch when the phone rang.

"Hello? Hey, Joe. Yeah, he's here. Hold on and I'll get him." Sarah turned around and handed the phone to Darren.

"Hey, Joe, what's up?" Darren said into the receiver.

"You wanna meet me at the airport before we go to the Carnival later? Say, around seven o'clock tonight?"

"Sure. What's going on?" Darren enquired as he stood up from the table to put his dish in the sink.

"I have a lesson today, and afterwards I'm supposed to stay and clean up the shop. Can you meet me then?" A loud crash interrupted him. "Hey, knock it off, will you! I'm on the phone!" Joe yelled, cupping his hand around the receiver.

"Yeah, I'll meet you there," Darren replied when Joe came back on the line. "Sarah will meet us at the Carnival at around eight o'clock. She's going shopping with some girls from school."

"Sounds good. Say, tell her to bring the girls along," Joe suggested.

Darren could tell Joe was smiling. "Alright, I'll see you at the airport at seven o'clock. Can't promise anything else, though."

Darren hung up the phone and headed for the door. "Well, have fun shopping with the girls. I'll see you later, kiddo. Oh yeah, can you take Bruce out again?" he added.

"Hey, why don't you take him along. I'm sure he'd enjoy hanging out with you," Sarah said, finishing her sandwich. She got up from the table, walked over to Darren and gave him a hug "Love you. And don't worry about anything. All is good," she said with a smile.

"Love you, too, weirdo. Okay, I'll hang out with Bruce today." After calling Bruce, he glanced over his shoulder at Sarah on his way out the door and gave her a wave goodbye.

A few minutes before seven o'clock that evening, Darren was driving down the road from the airport when a plane flew low over his car. *That's strange* he thought. The airport was definitely closed. In fact, Joe's car was the only vehicle in the parking lot. *Oh well, it's probably nothing.* He quickly dismissed his thought, pulled into the parking lot and parked next to Joe's car. He got out of the car and sauntered over to the shop where Joe was tidying up, right beside the main entrance to *Logan's Flight Centre.*

Even at that hour of the evening the sun was still shining brightly in the sky and the air was hot. The airport, which was usually humming with engine noise, was quiet except for the lone plane circling above. As Darren neared the shop, he saw what appeared to be a radio on a table outside. When he reached the table, he found a CB radio system and a note. Darren unfolded the note and read it:

> D,
>
> *Hey. Wanted to show you what I've learned so far. Talk to me.*
>
> *P.S. You'll need to use the CB.*
>
> *Joe*

Darren couldn't believe it. He quickly picked up the CB. "Joe! Are you a freakin' idiot?" he shouted into the CB. "What if your dad finds out?"

"Hey, Darren! Is this cool or what?" exclaimed Joe through the crackling CB transmitter. "It's okay, D. My dad's busy entertaining tonight. He'll never know."

"He's a parent! They always know!" hollered Darren.

"Oh, come off it! Don't be such a nag, man!"

"Joe, you know you aren't supposed to fly without your instructor or a co-pilot! You could get your license revoked before you even get one!" he warned.

"Hey, Darren, check this out! I've been practicing my spinning," Joe said and proceeded to roll the plane upside down then right side up again.

Oh, God, I think I'm going to be sick, Darren thought to himself. The CB was hanging limply at his side.

"Did you see that?" Joe shrieked through the CB transmitter.

"Yeah, I saw it," Darren answered meekly, lifting the CB to his mouth.

"Well, you have to admit it was pretty cool."

"Yeah, it was cool. Aren't we tying up radio waves or something? You know, in case other pilots need to communicate? Can't they hear us?"

"Naw, I changed the radio frequency. Not many pilots use these old transmitters anymore," Joe reassured him.

"Yeah, okay. But don't you think you should come in now?" Darren urged, as the plane dove towards the earth once again.

Darren rolled his eyes and clenched his teeth. "You must be breaking the law," he whispered into the receiver, fearful someone might hear him.

"Lighten up, dude. I'm almost done."

Darren understood the insanity behind his crazy friend's solo flight. (He just wished Joe had stopped to think that it might give him a heart attack in the process.) Joe was merely seeking praise for what he had accomplished. He had never received much praise or signs of affection from his father. What he did receive was firm discipline and quick reactions to anything he did wrong. He was seeking assurance that he had accomplished something good and that he would be a great pilot—not the usual lecture about it being his duty to carry on the family tradition. Joe genuinely loved to fly. Flying was in his blood; it came naturally to him. He was a pro and Darren was proud of him.

"Isn't she a beautiful plane, Darren?" Joe gushed. "I call her Domino 'cause she's black and white. When I land, I'll show you the domino I painted on her. She sure is a beauty and she flies like a dream, I tell you. She's a Piper Cherokee, a great plane to learn to fly in. You should try it sometime, or at least come up with me sometime."

"I'll check out the painting when you get your ass back down here. And, yeah, of course I'll fly with you when you get your license. I admit you're a pretty decent pilot."

Darren looked up at the black and white plane gliding above him. *It does look peaceful*, he thought to himself. Joe? Peaceful? *Now there's a thought*, Darren chuckled to himself.

"Thanks, D. That means a lot, you know. So what's on the agenda for this evening at the Carnival? Do you think we'll see any sideshow freaks?"

Darren smiled. *If only you knew.* "Let's just play it by ear tonight. I didn't see any shows like that last night. Haven't those types of shows been outlawed?"

"Maybe in some states. I'm not sure about around here. Why wouldn't people want to see freaks?" Joe paused for a moment. "Well, I think I'll take her in now. We should get to the Carnival to meet up with Sarah. After all, she's waiting for us."

Darren sat down on a bench next to the table and watched as the plane circled overhead and headed for the runway. Under Joe's expert guidance, the plane descended gracefully and smoothly. Joe seemed to know what he was doing. Just above the far end of the runway, though, he noticed that the plane was starting to shimmy and shake. Darren stood up and watched, wide eyed. He heard the engine sputter and then go quiet.

"Darren, I don't know what's happened! I've lost all power!" Joe shouted frantically into the transmitter. His voice sounded hollow and crackly.

"What do you mean you've lost power, Joe? Stop horsing around, damn it!" Darren yelled into the CB.

"Darren, I don't know what to do. I'm coming in too fast! I can't slow her down! I...I don't understand what's happened. This plane is perfectly fine. This just shouldn't be happening. I've lost control!" Joe stammered.

"Joe, can you pull up and circle around or something?" Darren asked, trying to remain calm.

"No, the steering wheel's locked. I'm going to crash, Darren. I'm going to crash!" Joe repeated. His voice sounded strangled.

The plane was coming in fast. It shot well over the start of the runway and was headed straight for Darren and the shop.

"Can you jump out?" Darren yelled into the CB.

"No! Oh, God, my dad is going to kill me. I need... I need help, Darren. I really need help!" Joe screamed.

"Joe, if you crash you could be killed!" Darren shouted. "There must be something—"

He didn't finish his sentence. Forced onto its side by the fierce wind, the plane had flipped over and was now plummeting at breakneck speed towards the earth. Darren began to panic. *If the nose of the plane hits the runway now, that will be it for Joe.* He stood frozen on the spot. He could hear the squeal of metal as the wind tore at the plane. He watched as the plane rocked and twisted correcting its position to right side up again. His heart was pounding so loudly he thought it would burst through his chest.

He knew what he had to do. He raised his outstretched arms in front of him, palms out, facing the horror. He could hear Joe's voice coming from the transmitter, but he couldn't make out what he was saying. It didn't matter—he didn't have time to respond to him anyway.

The plane, now only feet away from Darren, was coming in hard and fast with its nose pointed directly at him. He stared at it intently and gritted his teeth.

Chapter Six

-Impossible-

"*Stop!*" Darren screamed at the top of his lungs.

He was frozen in his tracks, holding his hands up in front of his face, his arms bent at the elbows as though he were trying to hold back a huge weight. The plane seemed close enough to reach out and touch. Darren closed his eyes—he couldn't bear to look.

Suddenly the noise stopped. All was silent. No more squealing or screaming. No screeching of metal on concrete. Darren took a deep breath and slowly opened his eyes. The plane was suspended in mid-air right in front of him. The nose of the plane was six feet off the ground; the tail was hanging in the air above it. It looked lopsided, nose heavy. The propeller was motionless, its blades a couple of feet from Darren's face. Darren's eyes skimmed past the propeller, over the nose and up to the windshield, where Joe sat petrified, peering directly into Darren's face. Joe's eyes were wide, his face a grim shade of white. He didn't blink or move—he just stared blankly at Darren.

The First Part of Trickery and Honest Deception

Darren cocked his head to look at Joe. Was he alright? Just then, Joe cocked his head to the side and covered his face with his hands. Darren's arms were still outstretched in front of him, palms pointing upwards just under the plane, like he was holding it up without touching it. He took a step backward. *That was crazy*, he thought. *I should level out the plane.* The plane slowly leveled out and hovered just above him. He drew in a breath and dropped his arms to his sides. The plane crashed to the ground. Darren had let his arms fall to his sides without thinking that the plane might follow suit. The plane appeared to be undamaged. His arms felt like they weighed a thousand pounds each. He felt tired. He closed his eyes and inhaled deeply. After slowly exhaling, he opened his eyes and picked up the CB he had dropped.

"Joe? Are you okay?" No response. "Joe?" Darren repeated.

"I'm okay, except for wetting my pants. What the hell was that, Darren? What just happened here?"

"Come on out of there and we'll talk," Darren assured him.

"Darren, I… I really need… I'm going to try and see if the plane will start now, okay? I just have to—" Joe's voice trailed off.

Darren stepped well out of the way and watched as Joe reached forward and started the plane. The engine fired right away and the propeller started to turn.

"I don't get it, Darren. It's all fine now. Everything is working as if nothing had happened! I could have died! You could have died! What the hell—" Joe was hysterical.

"Joe, get out of the plane. Please come out," Darren pleaded.

"I have to move it. It can't stay here. Dad can never find out. Never," Joe insisted.

"I know. I'll be waiting," Darren said calmly.

He hoped this next part would be easier. Joe just had to park the plane and they'd be in the clear. Darren watched as Joe easily steered the plane toward its usual spot on the tarmac. He noticed the painting of the domino on the side of the plane, just behind the wing. Joe had been right—it was really good. He took a few more deep breaths and sat down on the bench next to the table to wait for his friend.

Joe was visibly shaken as he climbed down from the plane. He walked over to where Darren was seated and sat down on the edge of the sidewalk. Darren got up from the bench and sat down next to his friend. He draped his arm over Joe's shoulder briefly before returning it to his side.

Joe looked down at his hands and shook his head. "What you did was impossible. The plane just froze in mid-air!" He looked at Darren quizzically. "How did you do it, Darren? You saved my life. You saved the plane and the buildings. I just don't understand. I don't understand what happened to the plane. What happened to the plane?" he demanded.

Over the next few minutes, Darren told Joe as much as he could about his capabilities and how he figured he was able to do it by the power of thought. He explained that these abilities had only just surfaced over the past couple of weeks and that he had no prior knowledge of their existence. He wasn't sure why they surfaced or why he possessed these abilities. He also admitted that he didn't know if he could stop the plane but had to try. He was thankful that it worked and that they had survived to talk about it. Darren told him that Sarah was also privy to this information and that Scott had witnessed his abilities before he even knew he possessed them. He apologized to Joe for not telling him sooner, admitting he had been afraid of how he and others might react.

"So, I'm a little—or let's say a lot—different from the average person. I wish I knew more about what I can do. I mean, I just stopped a plane from crashing and all I did was picture it stopping and then scream "Stop!" It's just weird. I'm sorry, Joe. That's the best way I can explain it. I'm just glad you're alright." Darren looked pleadingly at Joe, hoping he would understand.

"Oh, is that all?" Joe replied, looking at Darren and smiling. "You have superpowers. Cool! No, really, Darren. Thanks, man. You saved me and the plane. Dad will never know that anything happened. I'll just get one of the mechanics to look the plane over," He was back to his usual self. "Darren, I just want you to know that I'm a good pilot, really I am. I don't know what happened."

"I know you're a good pilot Joe. I have complete faith in your abilities. It's a big machine. There are bound to be glitches once in awhile."

"Planes aren't supposed to glitch, Darren. It wasn't a glitch. I can't explain what it was. It just felt wrong." He turned to Darren and gave him a punch in the arm.

"Of course it felt wrong. You could have died. By the way, I don't have superpowers."

"Oh, no? What is it then...Spidey powers?" he teased.

"No, I have special abilities, that's all."

They continued their conversation on their way to the parking lot.

"It's so cool to have special powers. I mean, it's like every kid's dream to be able to do what you can do," Joe said enthusiastically. "Hey, maybe you were abducted by aliens and they sent you back with superpowers! Oh man! That's pretty trippy! You're part alien! Sweet!" He was practically jumping up and down.

"I am not an alien!" Darren retorted.

"I'm just saying that I accept your new powers, no questions asked. They're pretty far out!" Joe said, opening the door to his car.

Darren unlocked the door to his car. "Just don't mention any of this within earshot of other people, okay? And don't call me alien or freak, either" Darren said coolly over the roof of his car.

"How about Superman?" Joe asked jokingly.

"Don't even think about it! We should get going. It's getting late and we're supposed to meet Sarah soon."

They got into their cars and headed for the Carnival. As they walked up to the front gate, Joe nudged Darren and motioned towards a group of girls standing by the ticket booth.

"Those are the girls Sarah went shopping with today," Darren said as he pulled some money out of his pocket to buy a ticket.

"Cute. Well, Sarah must be inside already 'cause I don't see her," Joe replied, stuffing his ticket into his pocket.

Once inside, they walked around and checked out the rides, keeping an eye out for Sarah.

"I don't see her anywhere," Darren said, mildly concerned.

"Me neither," Joe said, looking around. "Maybe she's watching the magic act."

They walked towards the magic show platform where a group of people were watching the show. The banner for the act read *The Mighty Marrion Lysbitt*.

"She isn't here," said Joe.

Darren spotted Vanrick Frulis in the crowd. "No, she isn't. Joe, I see someone I want to talk to. You can come with me if you like."

Darren and Joe approached Vanrick who, as if sensing Darren's presence, turned and looked directly at them. Vanrick smiled and nodded at Darren, acknowledging his approach. He walked towards them and met them halfway.

"I really need to talk to you," Darren said to Vanrick as soon as he was within earshot.

Vanrick quickly closed the gap between them. "I thought you might," he replied, patting Darren's shoulder. "I'll take you somewhere a little quieter so we can talk. Please follow me."

Vanrick waded through the crowd towards the tent behind the platform. Darren tugged on Joe's arm, directing him to follow.

"Darren, who is he?" asked Joe.

"He's okay. He's a friend, a mentor. He's helping me understand the changes," Darren explained.

They made their way safely through the crowd and entered the tent. Vanrick motioned for them to be seated. Joe sat in an armchair off to one side. Darren sat in one of the folding chairs that were already set up. Vanrick sat down in a chair across from him.

"What can I help you with?" Vanrick asked Darren. "And may I ask who your friend is?"

"You don't know his name?"

"Perhaps, but it is usually polite to introduce people," he said with a smile, looking in Joe's direction. Joe waved at him.

"Sorry. I just thought you would know him like you knew me. This is my friend Joe Logan," Darren said, nodding at Joe. "Joe, this is Vanrick Frulis."

"Are you a magician?" Joe asked.

"Indeed," Vanrick answered.

"Vanrick, today something impossible happened," Darren blurted out. "Joe was about to crash a plane he was flying. It lost all power and started to fall from the sky—"

"Oh, how terrible!" Vanrick interjected.

"Yes, but you see I stopped the plane from crashing. I mean, I froze it in mid-air only feet from the ground. It surely would have killed Joe and me and destroyed the entire flight center, too. How's it possible to stop a plane in motion like that?" Darren had risen from his chair and was pacing back and forth with his arms behind his back.

"It was incredible! It really was," Joe said, fidgeting in his chair.

Vanrick looked inquisitively at Joe. "You are a very lucky young man to have a friend with such extraordinary abilities, wouldn't you say?"

"I'd say he's my superhero. How do you know Darren? How do you know what he can do?"

Vanrick smiled at Joe and then turned his attention back to Darren. "Darren, it appears you are even more powerful than I initially thought. The ability you demonstrated with the cards last night was obviously just the tip of the iceberg, as they say. You are very powerful indeed. As for this great discovery, you may find that if your emotions are heightened, so are your powers. So much so that you may not be able to control them. You must be careful at all times." Vanrick raised an eyebrow at Darren and stood up from his chair.

"What ability with the cards last night?" Joe queried.

"It was amazing, exhilarating and extremely frightening today," Darren replied, ignoring Joe's question. "I didn't know I was capable of such things."

"It felt good, then?" Vanrick asked.

"It felt right," Darren corrected.

"I think he's part alien," Joe quipped.

Vanrick laughed. "He isn't part alien. He's flesh and blood like everyone else, and yet he's much more than that. He is gifted with powers the majority of people who inhabit the earth don't possess. He is true magic indeed." He turned to Darren. "Darren, there are seven basic principal effects in the world of magic: disappearance, appearance, transposition, physical change, defiance of natural law, invisible motion and mentalism. We like to credit the author Vincent H. Gaddis for his hand in outlining these principal effects for us. He helps others believe that magic is just good old fashion smoke and mirrors. However, all magicians *are* bound by these principals. You have experienced some of them already. I will help you understand these effects as you discover each of your abilities over time, if you should choose this path," said Vanrick.

"I appreciate that. Why was I born with this ability? Why not Joe?" Darren asked.

"Well, we understand this to be like anything else in the world. Why do some people understand trigonometry and others struggle? Why do some people get cancer and others don't? Why are people different heights? Why aren't we all exactly the same? It's just the way it was intended." Vanrick sat down on one of the chairs again. "As for stopping the plane today, I am very impressed. I never would have expected someone so newly introduced to his abilities to be able to do such a thing, especially without training."

Vanrick suddenly stiffened in his seat and looked at Darren. "I sense something is terribly wrong. You must leave now. You must go home," Vanrick said quickly as he stood up again.

"I can't. I'm waiting for Sarah."

"You must go home right away, Darren," Vanrick insisted.

Joe stood up from the arm chair and walked over to Darren. "Come on, D. We should do what he says. Sarah's a big girl. She can take of herself when she gets here." Despite his reassuring words, Joe looked concerned.

"Yeah, okay." Darren walked to the main entrance on the other side of the tent, away from the platform. "I'll stop by again tomorrow night."

"I'll see you then. Hurry, now," Vanrick said, waving them out the door.

They walked out into the night and headed for the main gate. As they approached Darren's family's home, they could see police lights lighting up the sky. Darren pulled over in front of the house and ran up the front stairs with Joe on his heels. He threw open the front door and entered the kitchen. His father was sitting at the table with his head in his hands. His mother was standing at the kitchen counter wringing her hands and looking very worried. When she saw Darren, she stepped forward and embraced him. One police officer was seated at the table and another leaned on the counter beside his mother.

"I can explain—" Joe started to say, convinced the police now knew about his near catastrophe with the plane.

"You know where Sarah is?" Mr. Whalley asked, looking up at Joe.

"No, sorry. I thought it was—"

"Oh, God," Mrs. Whalley moaned. She hugged Darren tightly and began to sob.

"What's going on?" Darren asked, freeing himself from his mothers embrace.

"Your sister has gone missing. The girls she was supposed to go shopping with today stopped by to see why she didn't make it. When I took Bruce for a walk earlier, he retrieved one of her running shoes from the bushes not far from here," Mr. Whalley said sadly.

"Are you telling me she's been kidnapped?" Darren asked in a strangled voice. He was on the verge of becoming hysterical. This couldn't be happening! Not to his sister. Not Sarah! What would he do if….? He couldn't bring himself to even think about it.

"First that poor girl Jessica Libben, and now our Sarah," Mrs. Whalley cried. She covered her face with her hands and wept.

"Yes, son, it appears she's been kidnapped," explained the police offer standing beside the kitchen counter. "We're currently looking for clues to help us in the search.

At least this time some evidence was left behind. We had nothing to go on in Jess' case."

Darren couldn't hear anything except ringing in his ears. His head hurt and his heart felt heavy. *Who would kidnap Sarah? Why would someone kidnap his sister?*

Chapter Seven

-Abnormal-

The next day, Darren stood motionless in the hallway at the top of the stairs, listening quietly as the police told his parents they suspected one of the Carnival carnies had kidnapped Jessica and Sarah. As they sat in the living room talking, one of the police officers informed them that the carnie had been spotted in their town prior to the Carnival's arrival and they had him in custody for questioning.

"I want to talk to him, damn it!" Mr. Whalley shouted impatiently.

"We're sorry, Mr. Whalley, but that isn't possible. We'll keep you informed as to how the investigation is going," one of the officers replied politely.

"Perhaps if he sees us he'll be sympathetic and return our girls to us," Mrs. Whalley said.

The police officers walked into the hallway on their way to the door. "We'll keep you informed. Until we find out more information, the best thing you can do is go about your daily lives the way you normally would. Trust me; in situations like these, it helps to keep busy." The police officer closest to Mrs. Whalley gently placed his hand on her shoulder. "I promise you we're doing everything we can," he said kindly, and turned towards the door. Mr. Whalley wrapped his arm around Mrs. Whalley shoulder as the police officers stepped outside. Then they closed the door and silently walked into the kitchen.

Darren sat down on the top step. *So it hadn't been just a terrible dream after all; it really did happen.* These sorts of things were supposed to happen only in movies—not in real life. And they happened to other people, not his family. His thoughts turned dark. He was angry and scared. He wanted to go to the police station and find the man who had taken his sister and his friend Jess.

Darren stood up and walked down the stairs. When he entered the kitchen, he saw his parents sitting at the kitchen table holding mugs of coffee. They managed to smile at him, but he could tell they were worried and exhausted.

Darren couldn't help but think about the carnie currently in police custody. His family's world had been turned upside down, yet the police didn't seem to want to hurt this guy's feelings. He seemed to be the obvious suspect. He wasn't from their town, so he had no business being there before the Carnival's arrival. Carnivals often hire ex-cons. No doubt this guy was one. The guy had come early to choose his victims. He picked his sister—a big mistake.

Darren sensed he was being watched. When he looked up, he realized his parents were leaning against the kitchen table watching him with startled looks on their faces. Darren looked around. All the cupboard doors were open and swaying, including the fridge door. The sugar bowl was overturned and sugar had spilled all over the table, as had all the coffee in the coffee pot. The chairs around the table were scattered around the room. When he looked at them, they began to shake and vibrate across the floor. He glanced at his parents and then at the cupboard doors, which were now opening and closing noisily.

Bewildered, Darren turned around and walked out of the kitchen. As he made his way down the hallway to the living room, the pictures hanging on the walls began to shake and bang against the wall. Mr. and Mrs. Whalley followed closely behind him, seemingly unable to comprehend the strange phenomenon. Upon entering the living room, Darren stood facing the window. His parents sat on the sofa. Suddenly, the armchair that was positioned beside the fireplace slid across the floor, causing Mr. and Mrs. Whalley to jump. Mrs. Whalley let out a yelp as she watched the chair slide right up behind Darren, who plunked himself down in it and stared out the window silently.

Finally it was quiet in the house. The three of them sat in silence for some time. Darren covered his face with his hands and wept. He hadn't cried since he had fallen off his bicycle and scraped his knee when he was a little boy. He still had the scar from that fall. He was certain he would have a different kind of scar from this day, one that would last for quite awhile as well. He slowly turned around to face his parents, who hadn't moved from the sofa. He slowly looked up. They were both staring at him—his father with furrowed brow; his mother wide-eyed and bewildered.

He knew his powers had run amok because he had worked himself into a frenzy. He knew better. He had been warned that if he became agitated or excited he might not be able to control his abilities and that could be dangerous. He hadn't intended to lose control of his powers like that. He had obviously lost control because he still wasn't sure what it was or how he was tapping into it, and he knew he would learn from this experience. He definitely needed guidance on how to better master what he was capable of doing because now he had to answer for his actions. This wasn't going to be easy.

After several very long minutes, Mr. Whalley finally leaned forward on the sofa. He clasped his hands together in front of him and rested his elbows on his knees. "Darren, I think your mother and I deserve an explanation," he said, looking down at the floor.

"An explanation for what?" Darren asked quietly.

"What do you mean *for what*? We were in the same room, Darren!" exclaimed Mrs. Whalley, who was now also leaning forward on the sofa. "How long has that been happening with you?" she asked with concern and sadness in her voice.

"Nothing like that has happened before. I think it was because I was thinking about Sarah and that guy the police said kidnapped her. My emotions were all messed up," he confessed.

His father stood up from the sofa and walked over to the mantel on the fireplace and stared at the pictures of Darren and Sarah. They clearly displayed their gradual transformation from plump faced baby cherubs to near adults. "What do you mean *your emotions were messed up?* What does that have to do with what just happened?" he asked, still avoiding Darren's gaze.

Darren shrugged his shoulders. "I think my being so upset and angry somehow caused these things to happen. I don't know. I didn't do it on purpose; it just happened."

"You mean it hasn't happened before?" Mr. Whalley asked.

"I already told you it hasn't happened before."

Mr. Whalley finally looked at Darren. "What else has happened?"

Darren looked at his dad nervously. He felt as though his father could see right through him. He would need to keep his emotions in check. "I don't know what you mean," he stated.

"Darren, stop playing games with us! What are you hiding?"

Why is it that parents always know when you're hiding something?

"Darren, we have always trusted each other. You have always been honest with us. Please, just talk to us now. We'll understand," Mrs. Whalley pleaded.

"It's nothing. I can handle it."

"Oh, no! Is it drugs? Are you trying some sort of experimental drug?" his mother asked, sounding distraught. Mr. Whalley sat next to her on the sofa again.

"Mom, it's not drugs!" Darren shouted. "Drugs! Why would you even think that?"

"You've always talked to us, but lately you've been so secretive, distant, not yourself. Not to mention what you just did." Mrs. Whalley looked at the pictures that were hanging askew on the wall.

"Drugs couldn't do that, Mom. You're a doctor. You know that," Darren said looking down at his hands.

"I'm a doctor who has seen people do some pretty strange things when they're using new drugs or combinations of drugs—horrible stuff. Too often these poor individuals don't live to see the next day or their brains are so obliterated they never leave the hospital. Look, right now I'm just trying to make sense of what your father and I have just witnessed. We need to have answers, Darren."

She paused for a moment and Darren saw a shadow pass over her face. "Oh, no! Oh, Clark," Mrs. Whalley said, turning to Mr. Whalley on the sofa, a look of sheer terror on her face. "I've heard of things like this with people who... who have... What if it's a tumor?" she said in a hushed voice. "Oh, God! He might have a brain tumor! We have to go to the hospital right away. We'll take him to see the neurosurgeon," Mrs. Whalley said, choking back tears as she looked at her husband and then her son.

"I don't have a brain tumor, Mom. Don't worry, it's nothing like that. I'm just different. I'm just not the same as I used to be," Darren said, deciding it was time to explain to his parents what had been happening to him. He proceeded to tell them everything, including the most recent event with Joe and his meeting Vanrick Frulis.

"Bullcrap! This is crazy! You're abnormal. There has to be a rational explanation for this, something that can be proven scientifically. Lauryn, talk some sense into your son!" Mr. Whalley bellowed. His face was a bright crimson as he nervously paced back and forth on the carpet.

"I've told you the truth. I've told you as much as I know. You can believe it or not," Darren stated flatly.

"We'll run some tests, that's what we'll do. I'm sure there's an explanation for this. Don't worry, son, everything will be just fine," Mrs. Whalley said soothingly as she walked over to Darren and put her arms around him.

Darren decided to just leave it at that. He wasn't going to argue. He knew that as parents they would stop at nothing to find a reason for what was happening. They needed undeniable proof that something had caused this phenomenon. They needed to find out why these strange abilities had surfaced. He had to admit that he, too, wanted some answers. He knew all too well, however, that the tests wouldn't reveal the answers they were seeking.

Chapter Eight

-Help-

Later that afternoon, Darren left the house to meet his father at the shop. He figured working would take his mind off things for awhile. He had persuaded his parents to hold off on the tests, as they all had enough on their minds with Sarah's disappearance.

When Darren arrived, the atmosphere in the shop was very somber. Mr. Whalley was listening to classical music. Darren smirked at his father as he approached him at the front counter. His father looked away and walked to his office. After a few minutes, his father came out of the office and put a couple of books on one of the bookshelves. Darren felt uncomfortable with the awkward silence between them. Afterwards, his father stood still in the same spot staring down at the floor. When he finally looked up, he looked blankly at the books before him on the shelf.

"Darren, I'm going to find out if the police have any more news. They might know more than they did this morning. Maybe I can help or something. You're in charge of the shop. I'll see you at home later." Without making eye contact with Darren, he turned around and walked out the door.

Darren walked to the office and changed the CD in the DVD player to something a bit more upbeat. He kept himself busy by dusting the shelves and re-arranging the display cases. He was wiping down the glass doors on one of the upright display cases in the centre of the shop when he noticed his vision starting to blur. He tried to focus on a pair of antique glasses in the case, but they were blurry, too. He rubbed at his eyes and glanced around the shop. The sensation was strange—it felt as though he were looking through gauze. He could see a vague outline of a road flanked by trees, in addition to what was in the store. He was seeing double images—one on top of the other, both distorted by the gauze. When he closed his eyes, he could make out the road and the trees more clearly. Keeping his eyes closed, he looked down and stumbled backwards, bumping into a shelving unit. He dropped the cloth he had been holding and reached up with both hands to pull the blindfold from his eyes, but there was nothing tied around his head. With his eyes still closed, he looked upward and gasped. He was standing in the middle of the store looking up at blue sky with a few scattered clouds! Then he sensed that he was moving.

'Get moving!' a male voice barked.

Darren's image of the sky shifted as he looked forward again through the blindfold over his eyes. He could make out a dirt road, a fence and the outline of a building. The building was in shadow but appeared to be leaning. Darren could hear birds chirping and feet shuffling on gravel. Without warning, his vision suddenly blurred and he lost his balance. Feeling as though he was falling, he suddenly realized that the ground was indeed coming up to meet his face. His fall was broken by a pair of hands that seemed to come out of his body but were not his own. The hands were tied with rope. Darren recognized the ring on the index finger of her right hand. They were Sarah's hands!

"Get up and keep moving!" the male voice bellowed.

"Where are you taking me?" Sarah demanded, sounding more angry than frightened.

"Move it!" the voice yelled.

Darren felt as though he was being shoved forward as the vision jerked forward. Now they were inside the building. He gazed downward again to see where they were walking. He noticed the worn wooden floor that was scuffed and dirty. The vision suddenly jerked again and the floor rushed up to meet his gaze. Once again, Sarah's hands emerged to break his fall. She was sitting with her back up against a wall. When Darren looked straight ahead, he could see the outline of a man standing in front them. Unfortunately, he couldn't make out who he was or what he looked like through the blindfold.

"Get over there with the other one!" the voice ordered.

"Get over where? I can't see, remember," Sarah retorted. After a slight pause, she yelled, "Hey, let go of me!"

The blurry vision moved to the other corner of the room. Darren was still seeing through Sarah's eyes. She still had a blindfold tied around her head.

"Put your hands out!" the man shouted.

"Why?" Sarah asked.

The man pulled Sarah's hands into view. As he looked down under the blindfold, Darren could make out a ruby ring on the man's right hand. Sarah must have tilted her head back to try and see it. One of Sarah's hands was scraped from her fall and was bleeding. The man cut the rope that held her hands together. One of her hands immediately rose to her eyes.

"No, that stays on," the man said, shoving her down onto the floor.

Darren could hear feet shuffling on the dirty wooden floorboards. Sarah's line of vision changed and she sat up and turned her head to the right. Darren tried to focus more clearly on the outline in front of him. Sarah stretched her hand out in front of her and touched something soft.

"Oh, no! Jess, is that you?" Sarah whispered.

Sarah's hand touched her face and Darren's vision in his left eye cleared. He could clearly see Jessica lying on the floor in front of him.

"Sarah, is that you?" Jessica's voice was very weak. "We should be quiet or he'll hear us," she said softly, her eyes still covered.

Sarah's hand dropped from the blindfold and Darren's vision blurred again. "Are you okay?" Sarah asked.

"I could be better. I don't know what he wants."

Suddenly the room started to spin. Darren was getting dizzy. He straightened up, trying to stay in control and not fall over. The vision changed and became clear again. Had Sarah taken off the blindfold? He was standing up, facing a rough, wooden wall. He looked down and saw Sarah. Everything went black for a moment and then the vision changed again. Darren was now crouched on the floor only inches from Sarah's face. Her eyes sprung open and stared right at him. Darren drew in a startled breath and backed up slightly.

"Darren, he's coming! Help us, Darren! Help!" Sarah pleaded.

This time her voice was frightened and her eyes were wide and pleading. The vision was starting to fade away. In the distance Darren could hear the unmistakable sound of shoes on the wooden floor. They were coming closer. Sarah's eyes widened with fear.

It was all over as quickly as it had begun. Again, Darren was standing in the middle of the store. He slowly walked to the front counter and sat down behind the cash register, unable to believe what he had just experienced. He had just entered Sarah's dream about what had happened to her. He had witnessed firsthand what she had gone through when she was first abducted. Jessica was with her and they seemed to be alright thus far. Sarah knew that Darren was witnessing her dream about the events that had taken place and had awakened to inform him that the kidnapper was coming. He was coming. Darren suddenly realized that the police had the wrong guy in custody.

Darren got up from the stool behind the counter and walked to the office. He opened up the closet and pulled out a broom. He might as well continue cleaning the store until he could figure out what to do with the information he had just uncovered. *How do you go to the police and tell them that the guy they have in custody isn't the guy who kidnapped his sister?* How could he possibly explain what had just happened? He knew the answer to that—you don't tell anyone. He doubted very much that his parents could handle this new discovery about his ever-changing personality. He had to think of a way to let the police know they had the wrong guy and that they should continue their search for Sarah.

He bent over to pick up the cloth he had dropped and then walked over to the display case to pick up the Windex bottle he had left on the floor. As he was walking to the office to put away the cloth and bottle in the broom closet, the phone rang. He hurried over to the phone.

"Hello. Whalley's Treasures and Peculiar Treats. How can I help you?"

"Darren, it's Mom," she replied anxiously.

"Mom? What's wrong?"

"Is your father there?"

"No, he went to the police station."

"He'll find out soon enough then," Mrs. Whalley said.

"Find out what?"

"The kidnapper they had in custody is gone!" Mrs. Whalley wailed.

"He's gone?" Darren asked, incredulous. "But how?"

"They don't know. They had him locked in the room where they were questioning him. When they returned to the room, he was gone."

"Gone? What do you mean *gone*?" Darren asked.

"Just gone. The door was still locked from the outside. There was no possible way he could have gotten out unless someone had let him out and then locked the door again."

"That just isn't possible. No one would do that." He suddenly had a thought. "What time did this happen?"

"It only just happened. The police called me right away. I'm leaving work now and heading home. The police are going to post a man outside our home for the next little while until they find the kidnapper again. Well, I need to try and reach your father. I'll try his cell phone. I'll see you at home. Bye," she said, hanging up the phone.

What a strange day this was turning out to be! Perhaps the man the police had in custody was the actual kidnapper after all. It just wasn't possible that while Sarah had been communicating with him, the kidnapper had somehow managed to escape and return to where he was holding Sarah and Jessica captive. Not if it had only just happened. Darren wasn't sure about anything anymore. He felt very confused. He wanted to find this guy himself but he didn't have enough clues to know where to start looking.

Darren's thoughts were interrupted as the door to the store opened and Joe walked in. "Hey, there's my special friend," Joe joked as he approached Darren.

"Joe, I asked you not to mention that in public," Darren scolded him as he put the broom back in the closet.

Joe looked around the store. "Relax. There isn't anyone in here. You know, people with a handicap or an exceptional gift are considered special. Some people might view your special abilities as a handicap. So that makes you my special friend. Besides, who else would know what I mean?" He sat down on a stool in front of the counter, smiling smugly to himself.

"I'm not handicapped and I don't have a handicap," Darren said flatly.

"No, you just have special abilities. Sorry, but I still don't see any difference. Special is special," he said, shrugging his shoulders.

"Fine, then. Whatever! Do you have to be so irritating?"

"I'm not irritating, am I? I mean, I just thought I was quirky and fun. Not you, though. You're *special*," Joe teased.

"I've had such a weird day, and it keeps getting weirder," Darren informed him, combing his fingers through his hair in frustration.

"Not on account of me, I hope. So, what's happened?" Joe asked, putting his elbow on the countertop and resting his head in his hand.

Darren filled him in on the latest development regarding his abilities and the fact that Sarah somehow knew he would be able to communicate that way. Not that he was surprised—she had probably read a lot of books about it. He also told him that the kidnapper had disappeared from custody at the exactly the same time he and Sarah were communicating.

"I have to talk to Vanrick tonight," Darren said. He knew the Carnival would be leaving the next day. "I hate that all this has surfaced right now. There's just too much going on. He's the only one I can confide in and who can answer my questions."

"I can't imagine these things happening to me. It sucks that the only person who understands it all is getting ready to leave. It really sucks, man," Joe replied sympathetically.

"Yeah, it's pretty hard to grasp. Besides, my abilities aren't much of a secret anymore. My parents found out."

"Yikes! How did they respond?"

"Let's just say they think aliens have landed and I'm one of them. They want me to have tests done to see what could be causing it. Mom thinks I have a brain tumor," Darren said, rolling his eyes.

"A brain tumor?" Joe shrieked.

"Apparently, brain tumors can stimulate certain parts of the brain, causing strange phenomena to occur."

"You definitely are a strange phenomenon," Joe said with a chuckle.

Chapter Nine

-Copper and Silver-

The door to the store opened and in walked a lady who stalked through the shop, cruising up and down the aisles and looking in the display cases. She reminded Joe of a dancer with her long legs and delicate bone structure. Joe remained seated at the counter and watched as Darren went to help the lady find what she was looking for. Darren removed several items from a display case so she could inspect them more closely. Eventually, she selected a very old brooch and a book from the upstairs part of the store. Darren wrapped the items and bagged them for her. She thanked him for his help, smiled at Joe and walked out of the store with her purchases.

"Finally, it's time to close up," Darren announced wearily. "Joe, will you flip the sign in the door?"

"Sure, it's the least I can do," Joe answered. He hopped off the stool and walked over to the door. He looked outside at the quiet streets and flipped the sign to *Closed*.

After cashing out and stashing the day's earnings in a bank deposit pouch, Darren came out from behind the counter and strode to the office where he turned off the music and switched off the lights in the store.

"You ready to cruise?" Darren asked, emerging from the office.

"Absolutely."

Out of the corner of his eye Darren could see a crack of light coming from the upper level of the store. Because it was tucked away, the upstairs section was always darker than the rest of the store when the lights were off. Darren stood at the bottom of the stair and squinted in an attempt to see where the light was coming from—a narrow crack at the top of a display case. He climbed a few steps to have a closer look.

"Joe, do you see that?" Darren asked.

"See what?" Joe was straining to see what up those stairs had Darren so intrigued.

"That light up there. It looks like something's behind that display case."

"You're cracking up. I don't see anything," Joe answered, following Darren up the stairs.

"It looks like a door," Darren said, as he slowly mounted the steps.

"Why would there be a door behind the display case? And why would you guys not have noticed it before," Joe asked, puzzled.

"Because it's never glowed before," Darren said, inspecting the display case.

"Yeah, I already said I couldn't see any glowing. See? There's no light. Nothing. It's just dark," Joe declared.

"Help me move this case," Darren said, bracing himself against the case.

"D, that case doesn't even sit on the floor. Haven't you noticed? Actually, that's weird," Joe said, getting down on his hands and knees to peer underneath it. "You guys obviously didn't move these cases when your father bought this place."

"We only moved the stuff downstairs. This area is small. There was no reason to move anything," Darren said. "We painted the downstairs and left the upstairs the way it was."

Joe stood up and helped Darren inspect the sides of the display case. "There must be a way to open this thing. Do you see anything?" he asked.

"Do these look like hinges to you?" Darren asked, pointing to the side of the display case that appeared to be attached to the wall.

"Yeah, it does. Well, if it has hinges it definitely opens," Joe said.

"Yeah, but how?" Darren ran his hand over the smooth sides and edges of the case, feeling for clues.

"Hey, can't you use your special abilities and say 'open sesame' or something?"

"I doubt it," Darren replied with a smile as he continued to inspect the case. He was eyeing one of the shelves when he noticed the tiled floor and its pattern of small crests embossed into the floor.

"Just try it! You never know, it might do the trick. Get it! Do the trick! I crack myself up sometimes," Joe said, chuckling to himself. He noticed Darren looking down at the floor. "Well, come on, what are you waiting for?"

"Alright, I'll try," Darren said, raising his hand and looking over his shoulder at Joe. "This is really stupid, you know," Darren said flatly.

"Yup. Let's see if my special friend can open secret passageways."

Darren closed his eyes and focused on the door of the display case. "Open," he said. Nothing happened.

"You didn't say 'sesame,' Joe informed him. "All magicians say that, you know," he snickered.

"Shut up, will ya!" Darren focused his attention on the door again. "Open sesame."

The case didn't budge. The light still shone through the thin crack on the other side of the case. Joe stood behind Darren, laughing.

"That was idiotic," Darren said. "Now, would you please just help me find a way in?"

"You know you can count on me. That was priceless, by the way. As long as you are capable of doing something I could never do, the least I can do is make fun of it," Joe added.

"Great! Knock yourself out at my expense," Darren mumbled, bending down on his hands and knees to look at the imprints in the floor. An imprint of a crest at the left hand corner of the display case caught his attention. It was different from the other crests in that it had two entwined snakes and a creature in the middle with the tongue of a snake. The other crests imprinted on the floor were all impressions of a stork.

Joe got down on his hands and knees to inspect the crest. "That's weird, isn't it?"

"Sure is. And look at how much more dirt has accumulated around it. Stand back, Joe," he ordered.

Joe stood up and backed away from the display case. Squatting down, Darren pressed on the snake crest, then quickly stood up and retreated to where Joe was standing. They heard clicking and hissing sounds coming from both the display case and the crest in the floor. With a final clunk and a hiss, the crest sank into the floor. The display case shuddered and vibrated slightly before emitting another hissing noise. Slowly the display case swung open to the left, the side where the hinges were located. Darren and Joe looked at each other, their mouths agape.

"Tell me you *did* see that!" Darren exclaimed, looking at Joe.

"I saw that," Joe said softly, looking at the open space on the wall.

"Can you see the light now? Can you see the door in the wall?" Darren asked.

"Sorry, I can't see any light. I can see the door, though," Joe said, stepping closer to the door. "There's no door knob or handle. There must be another secret way to open this door," he added, examining it closely. He tried pushing on the door, but it didn't open.

Darren stepped up to the door and placed his right hand on it gently. He felt a warm sensation under his palm and saw a faint glow. The door quietly opened outward, towards the secret room on the other side. Darren and Joe looked at each other in disbelief.

"You first," Joe suggested. Although curious to know what was on the other side of the door, he wasn't brave enough to lead.

Darren pushed the door open as wide as he could and stepped over the threshold into the cold, dank room. A glowing light emanated from a mysterious object sitting on a table in the center of the otherwise empty room. They both approached the table to take a closer look. The wand-shaped object, which appeared to be fashioned from copper and silver, was about eleven inches in length and one end was thicker than the other. When Darren picked it up, the glowing subsided. With Darren still holding the wand, they departed the now darkened room. The door closed behind them.

Darren further inspected the wand. He was right—it was made of copper and silver. The engravings on it were identical to the crest on the floor—snakes and a snake-like person with a serpent's tongue. Joe bent down and pushed on the crest stamped into the floor. Once again, the display case creaked and hissed before slowly swinging back into its usual position. Everything was back to normal.

"What do you think it is?" Joe asked.

"It's a wand. You can actually see this?" Darren asked, holding up the wand.

"Yeah, I can see it. Don't wave it around like that" Joe shrieked, stepping back.

"But you couldn't see it glow?"

"No, not at all," Joe confirmed.

"Well, now I have something else to discuss with Vanrick. We should get going. I want to stop at home and change my clothes." He wrapped up the wand and put it in a bag to bring with him.

"That was really strange, don't you think?" Joe said as Darren locked up the shop. After a pause, he continued. "You know, enormous walk-in vaults, not unlike this hidden room, were built into the walls of some of these old historic buildings. Are you going to tell your dad about discovering the room... vault... whatever it is?"

"No, he has enough on his mind right now. If it is a vault, then that explains why the room is there. But it still doesn't explain how the wand got inside and why only I can see it glowing."

They left the store and headed for Darren's house.

When they got to the Whalley house, they greeted Mr. and Mrs. Whalley and immediately went up to Darren's bedroom. Joe made himself comfortable in the armchair by the window. Darren put the bag containing the wand on his bed and reached up and pulled his shirt over his head.

"D, what is *that*?" Joe asked, pointing to Darren's chest.

Darren dropped the shirt on the floor and moved his gaze slowly downward towards his chest. What he saw made him gasp. A word had been scrawled in large letters on his skin. He dashed over to the mirror hanging on his closet door to better see the writing.

"Does that say 'help'?" Joe asked.

"Yeah, it does" Darren answered, running his hand across his chest.

"Does it hurt?" asked Joe.

"No, it doesn't hurt."

"What does it mean? How did it get there?" Joe asked.

"It's a message from Sarah. She asked for my help in the vision just before it ended," Darren replied.

"I guess she didn't want you to forget," Joe said with a smirk.

"We need to find them, Joe...and soon," Darren said, staring at his friend.

Chapter Ten

-The Keeper-

After Darren changed into some fresh clothes, he and Joe left the Whalley house and made their way to the Carnival. Darren was anxious to speak to Vanrick about everything that had happened in the past twenty-four hours.

When they approached the magic act, they were shocked to discover that Vanrick himself was performing on the platform. He was standing next to a table with a twelve-inch square block of solid glass sitting on it. A young boy had just come on the stage and was standing next to him. Vanrick asked the boy to empty his pockets on the table. The boy did what was asked and emptied the contents of his pockets on the table—bubble gum, a couple of marbles, a matchbox toy car, a small rock, ride tickets and his admittance receipt for the Carnival. As the boy held up each piece, Vanrick called it out to the audience and laid it on the table. Once all the pieces were displayed, he asked the boy to remove the articles from the table and put them back in his pockets. The boy complied.

Vanrick got down on one knee so he was eye level with the boy. "Now, would you mind showing me that little toy car again," he asked softly.

The boy reached into one pocket and pulled out all the items that had previously been there. The toy car was missing. Puzzled, he put the contents back into the pocket and reached into his other pocket. The car was missing from that pocket, too.

Vanrick stood up and looked at the audience. "Well, it can't have gone far. Has anyone seen this boy's toy car?"

The audience searched the ground and then looked at each other and at Vanrick.

The boy suddenly began to bounce up and down with glee. "It's there! It's there!" he squealed with delight, pointing at the glass block on the table.

"Why, yes, there it is!" exclaimed Vanrick. "Would you like it back?" he asked, his eyes twinkling.

The boy was speechless as he rocked back and forth with an ear-to-ear smile on his face.

Darren and Joe, along with the entire audience, watched as Vanrick stepped closer to the block of glass with the little matchbox car suspended in the center of it.

"Will he turn it into a cat?" Joe asked, staring unblinkingly at Vanrick.

"I don't know. Just watch," Darren replied.

Vanrick ran his hands dramatically over the smooth surface of the glass block, staring intently at the toy car. He placed his left hand flat against the top surface of the block and the fingertips of his right hand against the right side of the block. The area around his fingers began to glow. The audience watched with eager anticipation as Vanrick's hand entered the glass block, grabbed the little car and withdrew it. The glow disappeared once his hand was clear of the glass. Vanrick handed the toy back to the boy, who was now standing perfectly still. The youngster held the car in his little hand and looked up at Vanrick, wide-eyed and smiling. Once again, he was speechless. The audience erupted in cheers and applause.

Vanrick held up his right hand to silence the crowd. Holding the glass block at the boy's eye level, he asked, "Do you see an opening in this block?" The boy shook his head. "You may feel the block to make sure there are no openings," Vanrick instructed.

The boy ran his free hand over the smooth, solid surfaces. He looked up with an expression of pure astonishment, grinned at Vanrick, hopped down off the platform and stood beside his father in the crowd. Vanrick placed the glass block on the tabletop.

Vanrick surveyed the crowd and asked a lady who was standing to the left of the platform to join him on the platform. When he asked her to remove one of her sandals, she removed the left one, eyeing him skeptically. Vanrick took it from her and tossed it up into the air. The sandal never came back down. Neither did it hit the platform or remain floating in the air. The lady and the audience gasped. The shoe had disappeared before their very eyes.

The lady first looked at her bare foot and then at Vanrick.

"I suppose a pair of shoes would be better than a single shoe, right?" Vanrick asked her with a smile.

"Of course," she said, looking bewildered.

Vanrick raised his arm and then lowered it with the sandal, as though the sandal had been suspended there the entire time. He bent down to put the sandal on her foot. The only problem was that the sandal that he held in his hand was a lot smaller than the one on her foot, not to mention a completely different color and style than the one she wore.

"Well, isn't that peculiar," he said, looking down at the sandal.

Suddenly, there was a squeal in the audience, as a young girl got up from her chair at the mini donut stand and ran to the platform, waving the lady's sandal in the air.

"Ah, there it is," Vanrick announced as he rose to take the sandal from the young girl. "I suppose this one is yours?" he asked the ecstatic girl, who stood at the base of the platform wearing only one sandal.

Vanrick traded sandals with her and again bent down to place the correct sandal on the lady's foot. She smiled at him awkwardly, stood up and made her way off the platform.

"Well, that's it for me tonight, folks. Thank you all for taking part in the magic this evening," Vanrick said before bowing and walking off the platform.

Darren and Joe met Vanrick as he departed the platform.

"You know, you probably shouldn't mess with a girl's shoes," Joe teased Vanrick. "They get kinda weird about that kind of thing."

"Can we talk?" Darren asked.

"Should we go to our usual meeting place, or would you prefer somewhere else?" Vanrick asked.

"I don't think anywhere else is private enough," Darren replied.

"This sounds serious."

"You have *no idea*," Joe stated emphatically.

They entered the tent and took their usual seats.

"It certainly gets hot here at this time of year," Vanrick commented.

"Well, it's summer after all," Joe replied mostly under his breath.

"Of course it is. Understandable, then, isn't it?" Vanrick said. Joe grunted in response. "What's troubling you, Darren?"

"A lot of things," he replied. "I don't even know where to begin. It's all been so crazy."

Darren told him about Sarah's disappearance, that the police had a suspect in custody that morning—a carnie who had escaped from police custody that afternoon. He informed him that because of his lack of control, his parents now knew about his abilities and had not reacted positively to his confession.

"I am very sorry to hear about your sister. What terrible news. As for your parents, it's understandable that they would want to grasp onto the notion of a scientific explanation for what is affecting you. I can assure you, though, they will not find anything that answers their question. Tests will merely pose more questions because what they will discover does have scientific ramifications. Nothing to be alarmed about, though," Vanrick explained.

"I have to take the tests. I don't exactly have a choice, you know," Darren said in a frustrated tone.

"I understand that. I would never talk you out of doing what your parents wish. Ever since the scientific revolution, people have made it their mission to try and discredit what they cannot comprehend. Through tests and scrutiny they hope to unlock the mysteries and uncover things their feeble minds can't make sense of. Unfortunately, people nowadays don't believe in miracles and magic or that the unbelievable is a gift. They fear what they don't understand." Vanrick's eyes clouded and he became distant, as though recalling something from a distant past.

"My parents don't fear me," said Darren, rising up from his chair

"Perhaps not, but they do fear what they witnessed you do."

Darren walked over to a table and picked up a top hat. "I couldn't help it. I didn't even know I was doing it," he said, placing the hat back on the table.

"Tell him what else happened today," Joe said.

"Something else has happened?" Vanrick asked, looking at Joe.

"Something incredible," answered Joe.

Darren told Vanrick about his vision. He explained that he was seeing through Sarah's eyes but couldn't clearly make out the kidnapper or the surroundings.

"Remarkable! Your abilities are increasing daily. It's unheard of for so many powers to surface so quickly," Vanrick said.

"That's not all of it. Show him, Darren," Joe said, pointing to his own chest.

"Oh, we also discovered *this*," Darren said, lifting his shirt to reveal the word 'help' written across his chest.

"*Help*. This appeared after the vision?" asked Vanrick.

"Yeah. We didn't notice it until a couple of hours had passed. How long will it stay like this?" Darren asked, as he looked down at his chest. He was worried the word might remain there forever.

"I could make it vanish, but I think you should try to make it disappear on your own first," Vanrick said, rising up from his chair.

"How?" Darren asked.

"Just tell it to go away. *Think it*," Vanrick instructed, tapping his finger on his temple.

Darren nodded and closed his eyes, concentrating on the word, willing it to disappear. When he opened his eyes and looked at his chest, the message from Sarah had vanished. He looked up at Joe, who was smiling broadly at him.

"The word was self-induced by thought," Vanrick explained. "People who are clairvoyant can easily transpose such things onto their skin."

"But I didn't think it; it was the final image I saw of Sarah. She asked for my help. She left the message."

"Perhaps your sister stimulated the ability through your gift of being clairvoyant. She found a way to reach out to you through telepathy. This is not the case with others. The fact that the note appeared without your assistance makes you even more unique. It would appear that you and your sister have an unusual connection."

"We've always been very close," Darren confirmed, looking away. His eyes welled up with tears.

"Indeed. I hope I have been some help to you," Vanrick said warmly, placing his hand on Darren's shoulder. "Your parents will come around. Give them some time to accept the changes in you."

"Vanrick, there's one more thing," Darren said. He pulled the wand out of his bag and put it on the table in front of Vanrick. Joe got up and walked over to the table. Together, they told Vanrick about what had transpired in the secret room.

"So you see, V, I would never have found it because I couldn't see that the room was lit up," Joe said.

"It was weird. Only I could see the glow, and once the display case opened to reveal the hidden door, only I could open it," Darren said, smiling. He felt really good knowing that he was the only one who could see the wand when it was glowing.

"It revealed itself to you. It was meant for you to find," Vanrick replied, his eyes twinkling. "In the world of magic, we magicians are aware of a 'Keeper of secret knowledge.' The artifact was intended for only one very special magician after he or she had proven himself. There are seven artifacts in all, hidden in various places scattered throughout the world. Once the pieces reveal themselves and are collected, they will be brought together and provide answers to all that we seek—where we come from, the secret arts. Great power and knowledge will be revealed to the chosen initiate. Of course, this is all speculation. No one really knows for sure what the Keeper's agenda is. It is believed that once the artifacts are brought together, the initiate may become the next chosen Keeper of secret knowledge, but no one knows for certain. No one has ever seen the Keeper." He lowered his hands and gently picked up the wand.

"How can you be sure this Keeper exists?" Darren asked.

"The artifacts have this very powerful revealing spell on them for a reason—to select you for something very important," Vanrick answered.

"Where are the other six artifacts?" Joe asked Vanrick excitedly.

"No one knows where they are. The locations and the artifacts themselves are revealed only to the initiate. This one here is very rare. I'm sure you can tell from your experience working in antiques." Vanrick inspected the wand up close. "You may have noticed that you do not need a wand to do what you do, but you may still require this beauty. It looks to be from Egypt, perhaps 1700 BC. It's a metal wand made of copper and silver with engravings of snakes and the snake goddess. It is shorter than the ritualistic wand of twelve to thirteen inches; this one is approximately eleven inches in length. Do you see here?" Vanrick asked, pointing to the very tip of the wand. Darren and Joe moved in closer to inspect the clear tip.

"It is a crystal. The core is made of quartz crystals. This tool was created for attainment, allowing the user the ability to achieve evolution of their psychic and physical capabilities. Do take very good care of it." Vanrick winked and smiled as he handed the wand back to Darren.

"Cool!" was all that Joe could say.

Darren and Joe left the tent and headed for home. As they walked they talked excitedly about what they had learned.

"So, not only are you special, you're also the chosen one. What the hell am I? Just the sidekick?" Joe pouted.

"And a damn fine one! I'd take you as my sidekick any day," Darren assured him with a chuckle.

"That's great, but why couldn't I be special, too?" The only thing special I can do is burp the alphabet."

They had just left the parking lot and were headed for home when they noticed that the traffic was moving very slowly. They could see police lights flashing in the distance.

"Do you think it's just a roadblock? The police might be checking for people drinking and driving," Joe remarked.

As they slowly approached the area where the police had congregated, Joe and Darren were shocked to see a body sprawled out on the pavement near the ditch covered with a black tarp.

"Jeez, I sure hope it's no one we know," Darren said as they passed the grisly scene.

Chapter Eleven

-Oak-

The town was buzzing over the hit-and-run accident. People in cars pulled up next to Darren and Joe at stoplights and chattered on about the poor soul that had been hit by a car. Everywhere people were speculating about what had happened. The only known fact was that the victim was male. Who it was no one was saying. They overheard people gossiping that the injuries were so severe his face was unrecognizable. Darren knew well enough not to listen to hearsay; in most cases, the story eventually became so distorted, twisted and farfetched that it very hardly resembled the actual incident. Darren decided to wait and watch the news to find out what had really happened.

With so much crime happening lately, their town was quickly transforming into a big city. It was very unusual to have so many horrible things occur so close together. Darren's own changes were happening so frequently, too, that he barely had time to catch his breath. Before he could learn how to use and control one newly discovered ability, he had already discovered another.

This summer was turning out to be a real roller coaster ride. No previous summer holiday had ever been this chaotic. There was no question that Darren was intrigued by this new adventure; however, the gravity of Sarah's kidnapping hung over him like a dark cloud. He had made up his mind that he would try to communicate with her again. He was determined to find her and the kidnapper.

Darren dropped Joe off at his place and drove home. He went directly to the living room, turned on the television set and tuned into the local newscast. Realizing he hadn't eaten dinner, he went into the kitchen, made a sandwich and then made himself comfortable in front of the TV with a sandwich in hand.

"What are you watching?" asked Mrs. Whaley as she entered the living room.

"The news," Darren answered.

"The news? That's a first!" his mother exclaimed. "What's going on?"

"When Joe and I left the Carnival tonight, the police had a roadblock set up," he explained without taking his eyes off the TV set. "They were asking questions about a possible hit-and-run on Culver Road. We saw a body on the side of the road."

"A body? Oh, my! I hope it was no one we know," she said with a frown as she sat down next to him on the sofa.

"Me, too," he replied.

The news broadcasters proceeded to report all the usual doom and gloom stories of the world, which only confirmed why Darren disliked watching the news to begin with. The reporters' stories were rarely about fun and exciting events; they were always about death, disaster and catastrophe. If that was what the world was about, he preferred to remain naive.

Suddenly an image of Culver Road appeared on the screen. The police cars still surrounded the scene, their lights flashing hypnotically. The ambulance had arrived and a car from the coroner's office was parked alongside. The camera panned to pick up all the details of the morbid scene before focusing on the face of a young female reporter.

"This is Marsha Kendal reporting live from Culver Road. This was the scene of a crime earlier this evening," she said. "The police have confirmed that one male is deceased. An investigation into the cause of death will follow. The speculation is that this was the outcome of a hit-and-run accident. We will remain on the scene to report as more information unfolds this news hour. Please stay tuned."

After the commercial break, the reporter was back on the screen. She was conversing with a Police officer to her left. "Hello, we are back with more information regarding tonight's accident which claimed the life of one male. Captain Shepherd reports that the victim in this accident was a carnie from the Carnival just down the road from this unfortunate incident. Captain, would you please inform our viewers about what happened here tonight?" She jammed the microphone under the Captains chin.

"Ummm, well, it would appear that this could be the result of foul play. We will have to determine if this was indeed a hit-and-run. We do not have a suspect yet, as we are still investigating. The carnie in question, Mr. William Slip, was being held for questioning at the police station this morning in relation to the disappearance of our town's two missing girls, Jessica Libben and Sarah Whalley, until he escaped custody this afternoon," the Captain reported.

"He is the potential kidnapper of those two girls? And he escaped custody this afternoon? How could that happen?" demanded the reporter.

The Captain looked extremely uncomfortable. "That's all we have to report at this time," he said before abruptly turned around and walking over to the coroner who was speaking to the paramedics.

"I think our viewers would like to know how someone being held in our police station could escape custody like that, don't you, Captain?" the reporter pressed on, following behind him with her microphone pointed at the back of his head.

"Get that out of here!" the Captain shouted, pushing the microphone away. "That's enough!"

"We'll keep our viewers informed as the story unfolds. This is Marsha Kendal signing off from Culver Road," the reporter said with a phony smile.

Darren turned to face his mother, who looked pale and about to faint.

"Darren, if the kidnapper is dead, how will we find Sarah?" she asked meekly. When she turned slowly to face him, all the color had drained from her face.

"I don't know," he replied, looking down at his hands.

"How could this happen? What can we do?" she asked, her voice pleading for answers.

"I'm really not sure, Mom" Darren replied.

But he knew what he needed to do. He had to reach Sarah and try to find out where she and Jessica were being held, before it was too late.

Mr. Whalley walked into the living room and they filled him in on what they had learned. He informed them that he had been at the police station and had heard everything that was going on. He explained to his wife that the police might want to question the two of them about their whereabouts. They would also be questioning Mr. and Mrs. Libben."

"They think we're suspects?" Mrs. Whalley asked.

"Well, our two families are the only ones besides the Carnival who had any real connection to this guy," Mr. Whalley explained. "I guess we'll find out more later."

Darren excused himself and went upstairs to bed. Once he was in his room with the door closed and the lights out, he flopped down on his bed. With his arms up and crossed behind his head, he closed his eyes and thought about Sarah, silently calling out her name over and over again. He could feel himself spinning and falling, twisting and turning...

He was standing in the now familiar wooden, rundown building. He was looking down at Sarah, who was sitting cross-legged on the floor with Jessica, their hands tied together behind their backs. Their feet were also bound, but their eyes were no longer covered.

"Darren, it's so good to see you!" Sarah said with a smile.

"You've found us!" Jessica shrieked.

"Well, not exactly. She can see me?" Darren asked Sarah.

"Apparently," she answered.

"Jess, it's really hard to explain, but I'm not really there—at least not in physical form. I can see, hear and smell things, but I can't touch or be touched. I can feel certain sensations, but that's all," he informed her.

"Oh, no, you're a ghost," she said, lowering her voice.

"No, I'm not a ghost. I'm just there in a different form. Look, I'll explain later. Right now we need to figure out where you are because the kidnapper is dead, and unless I find you, no one will," Darren said sadly.

"The kidnapper isn't dead, Darren." Sarah informed him, as she tried to wiggle free from her restraints.

"What do you mean?" Darren squatted lower so he was at the same level as the girls.

"The dead guy must be the one who brought us food and made sure we were okay—" Jessica began.

"There's more than one?" Darren interjected.

"Yeah, more than one. We've never seen the one who kidnapped us. It's weird. It's like he's invisible or something,"

107

Sarah continued with a slight tremor in her voice. "It felt like we were being watched. We remember seeing a blurry image streak right up to us really fast. Then something pricked our arms and we felt lightheaded. When I awoke, I was lying on the ground outside with my eyes covered. When I stood up, I was forced to walk to this place."

Jessica looked at Darren, on the verge of tears. "It was the same for me. We never really saw him. He made the other guy feed us, and he didn't seem to mind that we could see him."

"I think the mean one killed the other one. We overheard them arguing," said Sarah.

"What did they talk about?" Darren asked, checking over his shoulder to make sure the kidnapper wasn't approaching.

"Getting rid of us once they got something from you," Jessica told him. Her voice had turned icy.

"Something from me? What do I have to do with this?" he asked.

"Everything, we think," Sarah said. "They were fighting. The mean one said he was told you finally found it, and that once they took it from you they were going to get rid of us."

"That's when the other one said he wouldn't hurt us, and that this wasn't about us; it was about getting the artifact. What do they mean, Darren? What artifact?" Jessica asked.

"I know exactly what they're after. It sounds like there might be someone else involved. You said the mean one was given some information. That means there is someone else. I still have the artifact, but I don't know where you are," Darren said ruefully.

"The argument got pretty heated, Darren," Sarah continued. "The mean one insisted that we must never be found once the artifact was retrieved from 'the girl's brother.' That's how we knew it was you. I figured it must be about one of the antiques Dad picked up somewhere. The other one said he would have nothing to do with it, that he was already a suspect and that the police were looking for him now, since the mean one had teleported him out of the police station. He said that if they let us go, the police wouldn't care if they found him or not."

"That's when the mean one asked him if he had ever heard of the term scapegoat," Jessica piped up. "After that, there was a loud cracking noise and this place started to shake. It made my hair stand up on end. There was a scream, a thump and then silence."

"He was framing the other one?" Darren asked.

"That's exactly what it sounded like," said Sarah.

"Great. What did he mean by *teleport*?" Darren asked.

"We think that was why we never saw the kidnapper. He can teleport objects, including himself," Sarah said, raising an eyebrow.

"This just keeps getting better," Darren said, rising to his feet. "I have to look around and figure out where you are. I may have to leave, but don't worry, I'll be back," he said, turning around to get a better look at the place.

"Darren, when I first got here and the mean one was pushing me inside, I fell down just inside the door. On the ground I brushed something with my hand. It was a sign. I could make out only one word—*Oak*," Jessica told him.

"I'll look for it," Darren said as he walked around.

There was very little light so it was difficult to make out his surroundings. After awhile, his eyes became accustomed to the dim light. It looked as though he was in a shed or very small barn. It was dirty and musty. On the other side of the room, he found a doorway leading into another slightly larger room where the front entrance was visible. He noticed the front door was slightly ajar. Cables hung precariously from the wall. A large support beam had toppled onto the ground on the far side of the room. The three other support beams were still intact.

Darren had noticed another closed door behind the fallen beam. When he walked over to the door, he saw that it was made of metal and had a large rusty chain and padlock. He squatted down take a closer look at a hard hat lying on the floor. It was very dirty and had a light on the front of it. He bent closer to it so he could see it better. He could barely make out some writing under the dirt. He squinted and the letters under the dirt started to reveal a blurry word.

Suddenly he stiffened and the hair on the back of his neck stood up. He could hear someone walking outside. He walked over to the partly-opened door. Peering outside, he saw nothing at first, but then a figure stepped into view. The figure turned towards him. Darren stumbled backwards as the mean kidnapper glared at him with a sinister smile on his face...

Darren's eyes sprung open and he sat bolt upright in bed. He was breathing heavily like he had just run for his life. He had seen the kidnappers face, he had seen it somewhere before, but Darren couldn't remember where. Darren's skin prickled again like it did when the kidnapper had looked right at him and smiled. He pulled his knees up to his chest, wrapped his arms around them and gently rocked back and forth as he contemplated what to do next.

He thought about the man's smile and how the hair on his neck was still standing on end. He was lifting his right arm to rub his neck when he saw it. Etched on the inside of his right forearm was the word *Oak*.

Still partly dressed, Darren hopped off his bed, put on a long-sleeved shirt and crept out of his bedroom. He sneaked out the front door, ran to his car, climbed into the driver's seat and drove to Joe's house. While standing outside Joe's bedroom in the basement of the house, he noticed the window was open, so he invited himself in. While climbing in, he bumped his head on the window, causing the glass to rattle. Joe sat up and reached for the baseball bat leaning against the desk by his bed.

"I'm gonna crack your head like a coconut!" Joe threatened.

"Keep your voice down," Darren whispered.

"D, is that you?" Joe asked, rubbing his eyes.

"Yeah, it's me," Darren said, flinging himself onto the bed. "I have to talk to you." He relayed what the girls had told him and described everything he saw.

"So, the guy saw you, then?" Joe asked.

"Yeah, he sure did, and I think he's expecting us to rescue the girls," Darren said.

"Yup, you can count me in. Did you see enough to figure out where they are?"

"Oh, I forgot. I have this as a reminder," he said, displaying his forearm to Joe, hoping the inscription would convince him that his vision had been real.

"*Oak.* Of course! Oh, man, it's so obvious! Why didn't we think of it before?" Joe exclaimed, jumping off the bed.

"Think of what?" Darren asked, sitting up.

"The old Oak Road mine! It's been shut down for, well, probably close to thirty years now. That's what it sounds like... the description, the partial name," Joe said, looking very pleased with himself.

"How come I never heard about this mine before?" Darren asked.

"My neighbor used to work there. I've flown over it a few times. It's old and decrepit."

"Okay, now we know where to go, but we can't go alone. The girls said more than one kidnapper was involved. We need help," Darren stated.

"Yeah, sure, but who could help us with *this*?"

Darren pondered the situation for a couple of minutes before it became obvious to him who he should approach. This person knew about Darren's abilities. He had also blamed Darren for Jessica's kidnapping. Darren suddenly felt horrible; if it weren't for his abilities and subsequent discovery of the artifact, the kidnappings may never have occurred.

Chapter Twelve

-The Mean One-

Darren had to run a quick errand before they arrived at their destination. The sun was just starting to rise when Darren and Joe arrived at Scott Firth's home—a white house with blue trim in the centre of a cul-de-sac. Darren had never been to Scott's house before; when they wanted to get together, they had always met somewhere in town. Joe, on the other hand, had met Scott there a few times so he could get rides to his wrestling matches at other schools.

Darren was nervous about asking Scott for help. "Okay, so let's go over this again," he instructed Joe as they sat in the car across the street from the house." You go and get Scott. Don't tell him I'm here, and don't say too much about anything. Just tell him you need to talk to him somewhere private and that it's really important. Tell him that you need his help with something that's a matter of life and death."

"Sure, sure, I got it. When we walk up to the car, though, he's going to see you. And there's no doubt in my

mind that after that, he'll punch me in the head," Joe moaned, staring at the house.

"I'll hide behind that tree until you both get in the car," Darren said, pointing to the big tree next to the passenger door of the car. "Then I'll come and join you."

"Well, here goes nothing," Joe said. He stepped out of the car onto the sidewalk and then paused. "So you think sneaking around to his bedroom window won't get me killed, huh?"

"Well, we can't exactly knock on the front door when it's just shy of five o'clock in the morning," Darren said, looking at his wristwatch.

"I suppose. Okay, going now," said Joe as he continued walking towards the house. "Do you think they have a guard dog that'll tear me up?" Joe asked in a hushed tone.

"Just go!" Darren snapped irritably. He climbed out of the car and hid behind the tree to wait for Joe and Scott.

Minutes later, Joe appeared from the side of the house, walked around the fence in the front yard and headed for the street. Darren spotted Scott drowsily rounding the side of the house following Joe. Scott yawned and scratched his head as he stepped onto the street. Joe got in the car on the driver's side. Scott walked around the car and climbed into the passenger's side.

"Get a new car? This one's nicer than that rust mobile you usually drive," Scott mumbled. "This one still smells new."

"It isn't mine," Joe replied.

"Well, that explains it," Scott said, stifling a yawn. "So, what's this all about?"

Just then, the rear passenger door opened and Darren climbed into the back seat.

Startled and instantly alert, Scott sat up and turned around to see who had climbed in behind him. "You!" he bellowed.

"Scott, we really need to talk—"

"Like hell we do!" Scott exclaimed, reaching for the door handle.

"Scott, get ahold of yourself and relax!" Joe demanded. "Darren will explain everything to you. This is really important. It could save Jessica's life."

"Save Jessica? What are you talking about?" Scott asked, looking quizzically at each of them.

"Scott, I need you to just be quiet and listen. This is going to sound absolutely insane but you have to listen and let me explain—"

"Well get on with it then, freak," Scott urged.

"You already know that I'm a little different from other people," Darren began. "I can do things that the average person can't do, and I only learned about this ability very recently. It surfaced very suddenly. That day in the locker room—you have to believe me—I had never done anything like that before and couldn't explain how it happened until just a couple of days ago. I've discovered that if I lose control of my emotions, these abilities can surface, and they've been surfacing a lot lately. I'm now learning how to control them and that I can develop more skills all the time. Last night, I had a vision about Sarah and Jessica. They're together and they're both okay, but it's important to find them right away."

"How do you know it wasn't just a dream?" Scott asked calmly, his eyes registering a glimmer of hope.

"It's happened before. The visions are real and the girls need our help," Darren said confidently.

"The news reported that the kidnapper was dead," Scott said, his eyes suddenly widening.

"That guy wasn't the only one involved. In the last vision I had, I saw the face of the kidnapper who is with the girls right now. We believe there might be another one but we haven't seen his face. Scott, according to the girls, this has to do with me and something I found in the antique store. An artifact. These people are dangerous and will do whatever it takes to get what they want."

"So that's what this is all about? Some antique? I don't care what they want. I just want to get Jessica back! Where are the girls? How do we get them back?" Scott demanded.

"Guys, this will be dangerous. You might get hurt, or worse. You might see things I can't explain," Darren warned.

"Well, the way I see it, we don't have time to sit around and chat. What are we waiting for?" Scott asked enthusiastically.

"Apparently, not a thing," Joe said, relieved. "Let's go kick some kidnapper butt!" Joe said as he turned the key in the ignition. "I'll drive. I know where Oak Road is."

"Oak Road. They're in the old mine?" Scott asked.

"Exactly," Joe replied.

"You saw that in your *vision*?" asked Scott.

"Uh-huh," Darren responded as the car pulled away from the curb. He sat back and tried to relax, thankful that the conversation with Scott had gone so smoothly.

"Do you think the crack of dawn is the best time of day to do this?" Scott asked. "Shouldn't we wait until tonight?"

"No, we can't waste any time. We have to take a chance and get them back right now," said Darren.

"I agree," Joe piped up.

They each had their own way of preparing themselves for what lay ahead: Scott stared out the window as they drove; Joe hummed along to tunes playing on the CD; Darren leaned his head back and closed his eyes, trying to remain calm...

He cleared his mind and tried to contact Sarah again. Soon he was back in the room with the girls. They were lying on their sides on the floor, asleep, with their hands tied behind their backs, facing in opposite directions.

He crouched down next to Sarah. "Sarah, is it safe?" he whispered.

Sarah opened her eyes. "I'm not sure. He isn't usually here first thing in the morning. It's morning, right?" She attempted to sit up but realized she couldn't move without disturbing Jessica, who was still fast asleep.

"It's morning, very early morning. I can't stay long. I just wanted to let you know that we're on our way. Be prepared, and wake up Jessica." He stood up. "Don't do anything stupid," he whispered. "I love ya, you know. I'll be seeing you really soon."

Sarah smiled before he opened his eyes. His neck was stiff as he lifted his head and peered past Joe and Scott to look out the windshield. They were travelling on a dirt road. With the mine closed, this part of town hadn't flourished the way the townspeople had hoped. But it was very picturesque, with tall, mighty oak trees flanking both sides of the road, majestic, snow-peaked mountains on the horizon and lush fields as far as the eye could see.

Darren was first to see the road sign leading to the towering, craggy mountain ahead of them. They approached the entrance to the mine with caution, checking for other people or vehicles in the area. With the coast clear, Darren suggested they park the car behind a tall, leafy tree so it would be hidden from view. They proceeded on foot down another short dirt road to the fenced-in entrance to the mine. After easily scaling the short fence, they approached a crudely built, wooden shack that appeared to be propped up against the rock face of the mountain.

"Jeez, it looks like it could fall over at any moment," Joe remarked.

"Is it safe to go in there?" Scott asked nervously.

"The girls are in there," was all Darren had to say to keep them creeping closer to the dilapidated structure.

"Stay close and keep an eye out," Darren said as he gently pushed the door open.

They stood back for a moment and listened for any sounds that would indicate someone other than the girls could be lurking inside. They heard nothing, so Darren motioned them forward. Having crossed the threshold, they stood in the beam of light from the open door and looked around, trying to make out the shapes in the room. They could see light in the room where Darren knew the girls were being held. He had no way of knowing if the girls were alone.

Darren's eyes quickly adjusted to the dark and he glanced furtively around him. Everything looked exactly the same as it did in his vision, except that the door to the mine no longer had a padlock on it.

"Joe, keep an eye out for anyone who approaches from outside. Scott, keep an eye out in here. The mine shaft door has been tampered with. We have no idea when or how this guy will show up. I'll go and get the girls. Be careful."

When Darren entered the room, both girls sat tied together looking up at him, wide-eyed. He couldn't tell if they were shocked that he found them or just happy to see him. He looked around the room to make sure they were alone. Luckily, they were the only ones there, so Darren walked hurriedly over to them and bent down to remove the gag from Sarah's mouth.

Wait a minute! The girls didn't have gags on them when he saw them in his vision only moments ago!

He stood up and whipped around, catching a flash of an evil smile. He sprang forward and ran to the doorway. Darren stood there for a moment and listened. Everything seemed normal.

In the doorway leading to the mine, Scott turned around to face Darren. "What's wrong? You look as th—" Scott started to say, but his words trailed off as he and Darren saw the metal door to the mine's tunnel open and witnessed a blur of movement rush in from behind it.

Scott was hurled through the air and thrown back against the wall away from the door to the mine. Darren watched as the ghostly blur rushed up behind Joe. Suddenly, Joe whipped around. He looked like a rag doll that had no control over its body. Scott stood up from the floor and he and Darren watched as the blurry image turned into a solid man right before their eyes. The man's right arm was locked around Joe's neck. Joe raised both his arms and tried to pull the man's arm away from his neck. He wriggled and struggled to get free, but to no avail.

"Did you bring it?" the man bellowed, his grip still firm around Joe's neck.

"Of course not! Do you think I'm stupid?" Darren retorted from his position in the doorway.

"It was stupid of you not to bring it. It couldn't have been hidden very well. Let's see, perhaps at home with Mom and Dad, or at the store, or at Joe's house with his parents?" he goaded. His lips formed into a sinister smile as drops of saliva dripped down his chin.

"What do you need it for, anyhow?" Darren asked, stepping closer.

"I wouldn't come any closer if I were you," he warned, grabbing Joe's arm with his left hand.

"Watch it! That hurts!" Joe hollered.

"*Precisely*," the man sneered at Darren. "Just get me the artifact and you can all go free. Otherwise, things could get pretty ugly. You're just a stupid kid. Why do you need the artifact? You have no idea what it's needed for, how important it is. I *need it*. You *will* get it for me!" he demanded.

"You'll never get it! Apparently, it was meant for me and no one else," Darren retorted, sensing he had angered the man.

The man let go of Joe's neck and with blinding force swung Joe around by his left arm and hurled him across the room. Darren heard a horrible crunch before Joe was released. Joe let out a horrific scream.

Darren could hear the girls in the other room screaming through their gags. Darren lunged towards the evil man, who lifted his left hand and shot a ball of blue energy from his open palm. The blast hit the open door to the mine on the other side of the room. The door exploded inwards towards them—past where Joe lay crumpled on the floor, holding his arm which lay awkwardly at an odd angle at his side.

"Scott, look out!" Darren screamed.

Scott ducked as the door flew overhead. Barely missing him, it crashed right through the wall of the shack. Still airborne, it flew across the dirt road and became lodged in a very large oak tree.

"Go get the girls!" Darren yelled at Scott, who stared in disbelief at the poor tree, which now had a metal door jutting out of its trunk.

Scott snapped to attention and ran into the other room.

Darren approached the man, who stepped closer to Joe on the floor. "Get away from him!" Darren ordered.

"You should already know that I don't have to be near him to hurt him," he sneered, glaring at Darren with a wicked gleam in his eye.

The man then strode towards Scott and the girls in the other room. He stood in the doorway looking over his shoulder at Darren for a moment before entering. Darren seized the opportunity to run at him with all his might. He barreled towards him and they both fell to the floor. Darren jumped on top of the man and punched him hard in the face. The man used his powers to hurl Darren backwards before rolling over and holding out his right hand. The shack began to shake and rattle. Dust fell from the rafters. Scott was trying frantically to free the girls from their restraints when a support beam nearby began to crack. They screamed, begging Scott to hurry.

"You're not fast enough!" the man hollered as he flung a blue energy ball at the base of the beam.

Darren sprang to his feet and held up his left hand, silently ordering the beam to freeze. The blue energy ball had already struck the beam, causing it to fracture.

Splinters exploded everywhere in slow motion, as if frozen in time. The great beam lifted slightly when struck by the energy blast and then began to fall slowly towards the three people crouched down on the floor below it.

The blue energy ball at the base of the beam was increasing in size and power. Darren quickly released another energy ball from his right hand and hurled it like a baseball pitcher's hardball at the kidnapper's face. The man jumped out of the way, but it grazed the side of his face and he fell to the floor. Yelling in agony, he clutched his glowing cheek with his right hand.

With the kidnapper temporarily out of commission, Darren returned his attention to the beam that was slowly plummeting to the floor. With intense focus, he was able to freeze not only the beam and all its exploded splinters in the air but also the ever growing blue energy ball. The shack continued to vibrate and shake from the powerful energy emitted from his beam.

"Scott, hurry and get them out of here," Darren yelled just as Joe stumbled into the room.

"Looks like I missed quite a show," Joe remarked, still clutching his arm.

Joe quickly walked over to the girls, ducking under the suspended beam and glancing up at the cracking rafters overhead. With his good arm, he helped Sarah up and they moved cautiously towards Darren. Scott pulled Jessica to her feet and they ran to the doorway. Once in the other room, they stood behind Darren as he addressed the evil man.

"I have to protect my family and friends," Darren said angrily through clenched teeth. "I will ensure you leave them alone and never hurt anyone again."

The kidnapper slowly stood up. Blood from his cheek trickled over his lips. He smiled menacingly, displaying blood-stained teeth. "I will get the artifacts! Too bad you won't live to see the day," he said, walking towards Darren.

"Get out of here now!" Darren yelled over his shoulder as he dropped his hand and turned to run.

Darren dove out the door-shaped opening in the wall of the shack as the base of the beam exploded like a firecracker. The top of the beam crashed to the ground. Splinters flew everywhere and became embedded in everything along their flight path. The rafters groaned, creaked and cracked.

Darren and the others, safe outside, watched the spectacle and heard the loud cracking and popping sounds coming from the shack. Then, after one final explosion, the rickety old shack completely collapsed.

Scott shook his head in bewilderment as he and Jessica sat on the ground next to the tree with the door stuck in it. "Did you *see* that? He appeared out of thin air. He was invisible. He was strong. He chucked those blue fireballs from his hand. *You* chucked fireballs. Things blew up and exploded. What happened in there? It's like we stepped into the twilight zone. I'm surrounded by *freaks!*"

Joe groaned in pain as Sarah tended to his broken arm. Darren stood looking at the shack, trying to spot the kidnapper or anyone else who might show up before they had a chance to leave.

"We should go to the car and get out of here," Darren said as he approached Sarah and Joe. He gave Sarah a hug and grabbed Joe's right hand to help him to his feet. "You okay?" Darren asked Joe as he stood up.

"I think I'm in shock. It doesn't really hurt anymore. I'm sure I'll be fine. Just a war wound," Joe said with a smirk. He looked pale, and Darren knew his broken arm needed to be set.

They all got into the car and Darren sped off in the direction of the hospital. Darren asked Scott to phone the police and let them know that they had found the girls, who were fine, and that the kidnapper's body had been trapped in the shack when it collapsed. Scott told the police that they were headed to the hospital and would give them a full description once they arrived. This would give them enough time to get their stories straight without including the supernatural events that had taken place.

When they arrived at the hospital's main entrance, the police were waiting, as were their parents, Jessica's parents and a news team. Darren helped Joe out of the front passenger seat and into the wheelchair that a nurse had brought for him. Jessica's parents hugged her and cried. Darren's parents hugged and kissed Sarah. The police held the news crew back as they entered the hospital. The doctors quickly checked out Sarah and Jessica to make sure they were alright. The police asked Darren how they managed to find the girls.

"Joe, Scott and I were bored and wanted to get out of town for awhile," Darren informed the police officer who was questioning him. "We figured a road trip would be good, so we got an early start. We happened to remember that there was a mine down Oak Road and figured it would be an interesting place to stop and check out. Luckily we did."

After the girls were questioned, it was Scott's turn. Every so often, Scott would shoot Darren a sideways glance. Darren felt uneasy and hoped Scott was sticking to their story: the kidnapper had confessed to killing his accomplice, the other kidnapper; the old entrance building to the mine had collapsed and trapped the kidnapper inside before he could explain why he had kidnapped the girls.

Finally, the police finished the interrogation and gave them a brief update. "Just this morning we learned that the kidnapper, William Slip, hadn't been struck by a car but had been murdered somewhere and his body dumped by the side of the road where we found it," said the officer. "With your description of the main kidnapper, we should have no problems identifying the body when we recover it from the mine. We'll call you after we bring him in. You kids did a good thing today."

After they finished speaking to the police, Darren and his family went to check on Joe but stayed only a short while because his parents had arrived. After thanking Darren and Joe, Jessica and her family went home.

The First Part of Trickery and Honest Deception

Before Scott left, he approached Darren and whispered, "Well, you're a good freak after all. What can I say? You saved our lives. I guess you're alright."

Darren and his family sat in his mother's office to celebrate Sarah's return. Mr. Whalley and Sarah were seated in the two chairs in front of Mrs. Whalley's desk. Mrs. Whalley and Darren sat together on the sofa against the wall.

"Darren, why are you wearing a long-sleeved shirt? It's summer, you know," she said, reaching out and pushed up one of the sleeves.

Darren didn't have time to respond before she saw the word *Oak* etched in his skin. Mrs. Whalley gasped. Mr. Whalley crossed the room and grabbed Darren's arm roughly to read the word. As Mr. Whalley held his arm, the writing disappeared. Darren was furious with himself for not remembering to think the word away earlier.

Mr. Whalley thrust Darren's arm back down onto his lap. "What you told the police was a lie, wasn't it?" Mr. Whalley barked.

"Some of it," Darren replied sheepishly.

"You're still doing that freaky thing, aren't you?"

"I really don't want to get into it, Dad. Look, I found Sarah and Jessica with that *freaky* ability. Can't we just leave it at that and be happy?"

"No, I don't think so! I'm glad Sarah was found, but what you are doing is unnatural. *You're unnatural.* You're getting some tests done right now," he said, pointing his index finger at him. "There had better be an explanation for this. Lauryn, make sure they run every test they can," he ordered as he stormed out of the office and slammed the door.

"Darren helped me through this horrible ordeal, Mom," Sarah said as she stood up and walked over to where Darren and Mrs. Whalley were sitting. "If it hadn't been for him, Jessica and I wouldn't be here right now. I'm just thankful it's all over."

"I know. Your dad's just having a hard time with this—not to say I'm not, but I'm handling it better," Mrs. Whalley said, standing up. "Well, we should get started on those tests."

Darren and Sarah followed her into the hall.

"Jeez, when did they find out? And how did they find out? Looks like it didn't go over too well," Sarah said.

"I'll tell you all about it. This may take awhile," Darren said with a sigh as they followed their mother out the door.

Chapter Thirteen

-Three Laws of Human Nature-

Darren's body felt like a pin cushion after all his tests were complete. By then, it was late afternoon, and rather than go home or be hounded by the press, he decided to go to the antique store. He couldn't wait to meet with Vanrick Frulis. He was eager to talk to him about what had happened that day. Darren stopped by the Carnival on his way to the antique shop. Well, it wasn't exactly on the way—it was actually a little out of his way— but he really wanted to speak to Vanrick, as this was the last night he and the Carnival would be in town. He had asked Vanrick to meet him at the shop at around five o'clock that evening. The shop would be closed, so they would have some privacy for their discussion.

Once Darren arrived at the shop, he kept busy straightening the books on the shelves upstairs. He was distracted by the display case that concealed the entryway to the hidden room. At one point, he stood directly in front of the case and gently touched the delicate glass on the door. He looked down at the snake crest imprinted in the floor tile to the left of the case. He figured it would be safe to take the wand out of the hidden room again, now that the kidnapper was dead. He was glad he and Joe had put the artifact back that morning. Since only he was able to open the door to the hidden room, he knew it would be safe in its original hiding place.

Darren opened the secret door as he had done previously. After crossing the threshold, he glanced around the dimly lit room. As he stood beside the table in the center of the room, he retrieved the wand, tucked it inside the waistband of his pants and pulled his T-shirt over it. He wondered who had built this secret room and why the wand had been hidden there. Perhaps the room had been used to store valuable artifacts and was only accessible to special customers. Neither he nor his dad had known about the secret room. It was hard to say how long it had existed in the heritage building.

He exited the room, closing the door properly so the display case completely hid the entrance. As he descended the stairs to the first floor of the shop, he heard pounding. Started, he stopped and looked around. It was too early for Vanrick to be there. When he looked over at the door, he saw Sarah standing outside staring at him with a puzzled expression on her face. She raised her arms with her palms up and shrugged. "I forgot my keys," she called to him from the other side of the door.

"Hold on, I'll let you in," Darren said. He turned the lock to let her in and locked the door again after she had entered.

"What are you doing here?" Sarah asked.

"I had to come and get something."

"The artifact?" Sarah asked, raising her eyebrows knowingly. Before he could answer, she sat down on one of the stools at the front counter.

Darren walked behind the counter and picked up his backpack that was lying on the floor. He pulled the wand out from behind his back and placed it on the glass counter in front of Sarah.

Sarah picked up the wand and studied it. "So, this is what it was all about. Why is it so important?"

"I didn't think anyone would come after us for it," Darren said. He told her everything Vanrick had told him about the artifacts and the initiate who was chosen to find each artifact. He also told her about the Keeper of the secret knowledge and how he might be a myth because no one knows him or has ever seen him.

"So how do you figure into this?" she asked.

"Because I'm supposedly the initiate, the one chosen to collect all the artifacts."

"What happens after that?" Sarah asked.

"Once all the artifacts are together, they're supposed to reveal great secrets," Darren said, putting the wand back in his backpack.

"It sounds like a wonderful adventure," Sarah responded, smiling from ear to ear.

"Don't get any ideas. I can't go trekking off to who-knows-where to look for a bunch of who-knows-what to uncover some mystery and maybe find a mythical person who probably doesn't exist," Darren said, taking a seat on the stool next to Sarah.

"Still sounds intriguing to me."

Darren turned around on his stool just in time to see Vanrick walk up to the door.

"Is this your mentor?" Sarah asked as she, too, turned to face the door.

"Yeah, that's him," Darren said.

"He's kinda cute," she commented, a smile tugging at the corner of her lips.

"Oh, *please*. He's probably Dad's age," Darren said with disgust as he walked over to unlock the door to the store.

Vanrick was dressed in a brown T-shirt and khaki-colored shorts with brown leather sandals. His hair was casually styled and looked somewhat unkempt.

"Hello, Darren," he said warmly as he stepped into the shop. "So this is the famous antique store everyone raves about."

"I don't know how famous it is or who would rave about it, but, yeah, this is it," Darren said with a chuckle and led Vanrick over to the counter where Sarah was seated.

"You must be Sarah," Vanrick said, pulling out a stool from under the counter and sitting down next to her. "It's a pleasure to meet you. I am so pleased that Darren was able to locate you. You weren't harmed in any way, were you?"

"No, we weren't hurt but we were pretty scared," Sarah answered honestly.

"That's understandable. I heard the kidnapper was trapped in the mine. Have the police confirmed this yet?" Vanrick asked, looking up at Darren, who was standing at the counter.

Darren picked up his backpack and placed it on the floor behind the counter. "We haven't heard from the police yet," Darren informed him.

"Well, I'm sure they have quite a mess to dig through," Vanrick replied.

"I hope the guy's completely crushed in there," Sarah said acidly.

"That just might be the case," Darren said. "I just can't believe they knew about the artifact before I did and that they'd kidnap Sarah and Jessica. Why would they want to harm my friends and family? I just don't understand," Darren said, shaking his head.

"It would appear that someone else is aware of your abilities and staged the kidnappings to bring them to the surface. The same goes for the unfortunate event involving your friend Joe and his plane," Vanrick added.

Sarah turned around and looked at Darren. "Joe and his plane? What happened to Joe and his plane? What's he talking about?"

"I'll tell you about it later, I promise," Darren assured her.

"Sounds like I missed a lot while I was gone." Sarah responded.

Darren addressed Vanrick again. "The guy, he was like me, powerful and strong. He did things I didn't even know I could do until I fought back using my own powers. Maybe he was part of the magic act. He was tall and had short, dark hair that was graying at the temples, high, arched eyebrows, blue eyes and the wickedest smile I've ever seen. Does he sound familiar?"

"We had a magician in our group by the name of Marrion Lysbitt. He's a long time friend. Sadly, though, he's unstable. You see, he likes to dabble in black magic and the darker side of voodoo. I've been worried about him lately. He left us without saying a word to anyone. He hasn't been around for any of his scheduled magic acts. Of course, this is only speculation; I'm not saying it *is* him. It's possible that the kidnapper was aware of the Keeper and the story of the initiate. Come to think of it, Marrion was the one who suggested the Carnival come here. Perhaps his powers had revealed your whereabouts and he needed to awaken your abilities so you would locate the artifact. Hmmm, very intriguing."

"But my abilities surfaced before the kidnappings."

"True. He may have tried to reach you telepathically, and when that wasn't working fast enough, he resorted to kidnapping," Vanrick suggested.

"Makes sense," Sarah agreed, nodding her head.

"I guess so," Darren replied. "This is all so crazy. Vanrick, I don't know what to do. My parents are falling apart over all this. They think I'm some kind of monster. I think Mom can handle it, but I don't think Dad will ever come around. He can't even look me in the eyes lately," Darren said sadly.

"Dad does seem to be a bit obsessed with this," Sarah agreed. "He seems to be genuinely disturbed by Darren's newfound abilities. Or maybe he's just worried."

"Your parents will adapt to the changes in you. It will just take some time," Vanrick assured Darren.

"I don't know. It doesn't feel like it. I feel so alone. I know I have Joe and Sarah's support, and now Scott and Jessica know about my abilities, yet I feel like I'm on my own without my parents support. I appreciate your guidance; I really need it. Maybe I should just ignore what's happening and pretend to be like I was before all this happened." Darren plopped down on one of the stools at the end of the counter.

"What about the other artifacts? You can't just ignore your destiny," Sarah reminded him.

Vanrick looked at Sarah and than at Darren. "She's right, Darren. You have a destiny to fulfill and you have difficult decisions to make. We all yearn for the support of others, but sometimes support cannot be offered because others can't fully comprehend the big picture. They perceive things outside the acceptable norm to be abnormal and may fear what they do not understand. Of course, the decision is completely yours to make."

"I don't know how to make them understand or not fear me," Darren complained. "I just want things to be the way they were. I want them to just accept me, their son."

"Mom and Dad will come around, Darren. Just give them some more time," Sarah said encouragingly.

"Darren, what you are feeling is completely understandable. People have had to endure such things since the beginning of time. You see, individuals react to persecution or oppression in one of three ways. These are laws of human nature. The reaction is the same whether you are a person with special abilities, a member of a minority, a man, woman, or child. Each person must make a decision. Darren, you need to decide which of these ways works best for you."

"I know—" Darren started to say.

"I haven't told you what the laws are yet. Listen carefully. I spoke to you briefly about this once before but now I will explain in more detail. Firstly, there are those who accept and conform to oppression and persecution without fighting. They avoid who they truly are and become what is expected of them. Then there are those who fight the establishment and want to affect change. They wish to grow and evolve. And finally, there are those who exploit their differences for personal gain, whether it be monetary or spiritual, to gain notoriety, or purely for attention. These individuals seek fame and rock star status. A good example of this is my personal friend David Copperfield. He knows what to do with his abilities." Vanrick paused to wink at Sarah. "Of course, this can be tricky. Some who choose this path—Copperfield, for example—seek personal gain for themselves without harming others in the process. But some others will stop at nothing to gain what they crave.

"So, Darren, the choice is yours. You are welcome to join us in the magic act. We have an opening for one more gifted magician. You may find this to be favorable— you are one of us, after all." Vanrick looked admiringly at Darren. "The crowd will love you and applaud you and your special gifts, as you thrill and entertain them with your talents in the art of trickery and honest deception. You don't have long to think about it, though, as the Carnival will be leaving at noon tomorrow."

"Tomorrow? That's too soon!" Sarah exclaimed, rising from her stool.

"Sarah, it's okay. I'm not going anywhere," Darren declared, standing up.

"We leave for Mexico City at noon tomorrow. Every year they have a spectacular Battle of the Carnivals. Many different carnival acts get together and try to outdo each other. It's a lot of fun. You really don't want to miss it," Vanrick said as he, too, rose from his stool. "Well, I really should be going now. It was a pleasure meeting you, Sarah," Vanrick said with a warm smile.

"You, too," Sarah said, returning the smile. She and Darren walked Vanrick to the door.

After Vanrick left, Darren retrieved his backpack from behind the counter and locked up the store.

As he and Sarah drove home, Darren thought about the three laws of human nature and tried to determine which one he would follow. He had many important decisions to make, none of which were easy. Should he live out his life as a normal guy and never again use his special abilities, or should he embrace his powers? If he embraced his abilities, would he remain at home and continue doing what he was doing, or would he also embrace his destiny and look for the other artifacts? Where would that take him? Would it be safe, or would more people get hurt because of him? Would his family understand? Darren knew he needed to consider all these things.

Chapter Fourteen

-Normal-

Darren and Sarah arrived home just in time for dinner. Darren walked into the kitchen and dropped his backpack on the floor next to the kitchen counter. Their mother was scooping some mashed potatoes into a serving bowl at the kitchen counter. Mr. Whalley was already seated in the dining room. Sarah went into the dining room to sit with Mr. Whalley to wait for dinner to be served. Darren crossed the kitchen and picked up a folder he found lying on the table.

"What's this?" Darren asked his mother.

"Oh, the results from your tests today came back pretty quickly. Mrs. Logan tested your blood and found absolutely nothing out of the ordinary. I brought the results from the other tests home to look them over more closely." She turned away from the counter and started walking into the dining room.

"Well, am I normal?" Darren asked impatiently.

Mr. Whalley looked up as Darren took a seat at the table. "As normal as any other teenage boy your age—at least that's what the results show. The only difference besides the obvious, which isn't necessarily alarming but is a little unusual, is that certain areas of your brain that aren't usually active are showing unusual activity. I'm happy to say that you don't have a tumor. Thank goodness! I was a little worried when those strange things started happening—you know, things flying around, cupboards opening," Mrs. Whalley said as she sat opposite her husband at the head of the table.

"So everything is fine? I'm not dying and I'm not overly unusual. That's good, then," Darren concluded.

"You're not dying, but you're definitely unusual," Mr. Whalley blurted out. "There *is* something wrong with you and I don't need the damned tests to prove it."

"I won't argue that something else's going on, but it won't hurt me or anyone else," Darren assured his father as he took his place at the dinner table.

"You don't know that for sure," Mr. Whalley said as he grabbed a bun from the bread basket.

"Dad, Darren has done good things with his special abilities," Sarah offered.

"Sure, I get that. That's fine, but he shouldn't be like this to begin with. I just can't accept it," Mr. Whalley said, looking down at the large dollop of mashed potatoes on his plate.

"Alright, all of you, there apparently isn't anything we can do medically to change Darren back to the way he was before, so we're just going to have to accept this change and move on and be supportive," Mrs. Whalley said. She turned to Darren and reached for his hand. "We love you, Darren, and nothing will ever change that," she said with a warm smile.

"I do love you, but I don't have to accept what's happening to you," Mr. Whalley retorted stubbornly. "These abilities are just not right. There's something wrong with my son and I can't ignore it."

"You don't have to ignore it. He's still Darren," Sarah tried to explain to her father.

"They must have missed something, I just know it. First thing tomorrow we're going back to the hospital for more tests."

"The roast looks good," Mrs. Whalley said, quickly changing the subject.

"More tests?" Darren blurted out. "Come on! I can't take this anymore! Dad, would you just get over it! How are we supposed to feel comfortable talking to you guys about anything if you're going to react this way?"

"You *can* talk to us about anything, you both know that," Mrs. Whalley said defensively.

"That's not the way we see it. Of all the people who would find out about me, I thought for sure my parents would be the ones who would understand and support me," Darren said.

"We do understand!" Mrs. Whalley insisted.

"Speak for yourself!" snapped Mr. Whalley. "I *don't* understand, and it's hard to be supportive when no one knows what's wrong with you."

"Whatever. I'm tired of trying to defend myself, and I'm hungry. Can we just eat now?" Darren asked irritably, plunging his fork into the roast beef on his plate.

After dinner, Darren went upstairs to his bedroom. He needed to be alone for awhile. He closed his bedroom door behind him, walked over to the bed, tossed his backpack onto it and sat down. He unzipped the backpack and pulled out the wand.

"What do you want from me?" he murmured, inspecting the wand closely. "Where will you take me? And when?" His voice reflected his somber mood.

Darren gently placed the wand on the nightstand next to his bed and lay back against his pillow, crossing his arms behind his head. His head swam with thoughts about his family and the events of the day. Why did his father have to make this so difficult for him? He was still his son and that would never change. Why couldn't his father see that? What was he so afraid of?

Lost in thought, Darren didn't hear the knocking on the bedroom door. It was a couple of minutes before he finally snapped out of his reverie and dismissed the dark thoughts in his head.

"Come in," he said.

Sarah poked her head around the open door and asked, "Are you decent?"

"Yeah, you can come in," he answered.

"I wouldn't worry too much about Mom and Dad. They'll come around," she said, sitting down at the edge of the bed.

"Maybe, but I wouldn't bet on it," Darren said. He sat up and swung his legs over the side of the bed.

"It's not that bad," said Sarah.

"Easy for you to say. You're not the one they—or at least Dad—thinks is possessed or something."

"I'm sure it will pass and things will be just like they used to be," Sarah said to console him.

"I don't know. I don't think I can live here like this," he said, thinking about his father and that strange, distant look in his eyes whenever he spoke to him.

"What are you saying?" Sarah asked, suddenly alarmed.

"Nothing. I'm just upset."

Darren and Sarah continued to talk, unaware that a police car had just pulled up in front of their house. Eventually, Sarah got up from where she had been sitting and wandered over to the window. She glanced down at the street below and saw the police car parked in front of their house. Her posture suddenly changed; her shoulders slumped and her head drooped.

"What's the matter?" asked Darren. He stood up and walked over to the window. Spotting the police car, he said, "They probably have news about the kidnapper. Don't worry about it," Darren said, giving Sarah's shoulder a gentle squeeze.

Sarah moved her gaze away from the window and turned to Darren. "I just want to put this behind me, that's all," she said ruefully.

"I know. Me, too," Darren said sympathetically. "Should we go and find out what they know? Maybe they need me to identify the kidnapper."

"I suppose we should. The sooner this is over, the better," Sarah said, walking towards the bedroom door. Darren followed her across the room and they made their way into the hall and down the stairs.

Darren could hear voices coming from the living room. His mother sounded very upset as she spoke to a police officer. He didn't like the sound of it. When they stepped into the living room, Darren recognized the Police Chief, Captain Shepherd. His parents, the Captain and the other officer turned around to look at the two of them as they stood awkwardly in the entranceway.

"Darren, Sarah," Captain Shepherd said, nodding his head. He looked tired and worn out. "We've spent the entire day digging through the collapsed mine."

Visibly upset, Mrs. Whalley joined her husband on the sofa and folded her hands in her lap to appear composed.

"We've gotten through most of the rubble in the shack and have opened up the entranceway to the mine," the Captain continued. "We searched every possible place he could be buried in there, but we didn't find his body. It's as though he just disappeared. I know that sounds crazy, but this isn't the first time it's happened." Captain Shepherd slumped down in an armchair. The other officer appeared to be distracted as he stared out the window into the street.

Darren wasn't overly shocked by this news, but he was still uneasy with it. Looking at Sarah, he knew she felt the same way.

"I've told your parents that we will post a couple of officers outside the house for the next couple of nights, and the two of you will have protection during the day. It's all we can do at this point."

"Are you sure he isn't in the mine somewhere?" Darren had to ask.

"We searched through as much of the debris as we could. Further down the mine is another huge cave-in, but there was no way we could get through that section. If we can't get in, you can bet your ass no one can get out either. If he made it that far back in the mine, he's likely disappeared and we won't be seeing him again. But just in case he didn't make it that far into the mine, we want to make sure the two of you are protected. Just for a couple of days, that's all."

"Let's hope he did," Sarah said, sitting down next to her parents on the sofa.

"Well, we'll be off now. Officers Jeffries and Boone will be just outside if you require any assistance. Have yourselves a good evening,"

Captain Shepherd and the other officer headed towards the door. Mr. and Mrs. Whalley walked them out while Darren and Sarah remained in the living room.

"Do you think he'll come after us again?" Sarah whispered.

"If he isn't in the mine, I think he'll eventually show up."

"You *know* he isn't in the mine. He can teleport," she said.

"I know. I just thought perhaps he was too distracted or hurt to do it," Darren responded.

"Maybe. We can always hope," Sarah added.

"Maybe...hopefully," Darren replied.

Chapter Fifteen

-Have to Go-

Flames from thousands of candles flickered, danced and waved in the night sky like tongues lapping at the darkness. The full moon beamed down on exuberant revelers, as they strolled with their animals. Stark white faces and bright white skulls with black empty eyes were scattered throughout the crowd. Pairs of men carried fluttering banners suspended from wooden poles propped on their shoulders. Vendors stood beside their carts selling brightly colored figurines and skulls made of pure white sugar. Women carried baskets of bread and toys. Giggling children darted through the crowd. Young ladies carried fragrant flowers and incense. Young and old, they paraded under the moon waving their flickering candles to the graveyard beyond.

Darren watched in amazement at the spectacular scene in front of him. He had never seen so many people gathered together in one place before. He followed the group through a courtyard where a tall mound of bones and skulls encircled the likenesses of a brightly adorned

man and woman. Darren was certain the figures represented important people but found it strange that they would be surrounded by skulls and bones.

As Darren made his way to the cemetery, he was overwhelmed by the alluring aromas—flowers, incense, coffee, spices and food. The burial plots in the cemetery had been decorated with marigolds, tiny pumpkins, pictures and candles. Some were even adorned with breads, tequila bottles, candy skulls with names on them, fruit, baby rattles and toys. People sat on blankets in family groups, eager to enjoy the food spread out before them.

The graveyard was buzzing with song, chatter and activity. For such a traditionally grim place, the atmosphere was particularly light and happy. A place that was typically cold and dead was warm and alive this night. Instead of being dark and gloomy, it was bright and welcoming. Darren looked around him and took in all the sights, sounds and aromas. He noticed a little girl sitting playing with a toy truck beside a tombstone. A banner draped over one side of the tombstone read *Angelitos. Perhaps her brother, he thought.*

As he walked towards the central courtyard, where most of the activity was taking place, he could hear cracks and pops ringing out through the night. When he looked upward along with the crowd, he saw small firecrackers explode in a rainbow of colors. People applauded and cheered, and the children danced and laughed beneath the painted sky.

Darren smiled. He was lost in this fantasy world, the strange events of the day momentarily forgotten. When he gazed at the crowd, his eyes were drawn to a family directly across from him. A little boy jumped up and down excitedly in front of his father, his arms outstretched. The father stepped forward and then crouched down to pick up the boy. Darren's eyes followed the man as he bent forward and hoisted his son up, then returned to the spot where he had previously been standing. Suddenly, Darren's heart began pounding loudly in his throat. He couldn't swallow and his throat felt constricted. Standing before him was a man with a disfiguring scar down the left side of his face, the inflamed flesh raised and raw. Certain that Darren had seen him, the man put on his evilest smile.

Marrion Lysbitt moved forward at precisely the same moment the father and his son stepped back into place. After shoving the father and his son out of his way, Marrion strode purposefully towards Darren, extending his left arm to emit a blue energy ball from his palm. Darren reacted quickly to avoid being hit. The energy ball struck a vendor's cart directly behind where he had been standing, causing it to burst apart and send candy skulls flying towards the street. In one swift, blurry motion, Marrion Lysbitt spun around and seemingly disappeared, then instantly reappeared with his hand clenched around Darren's throat.

"I will destroy you," Marrion sneered through gritted teeth. As he leaned in uncomfortably close, Darren could feel his fetid breath on his face. Marrion's eyes flamed like the fires of Hell, pure hatred seared into his very soul. He glowered at Darren as his hand tightened around Darren's throat.

Darren's eyes sprang open. He quickly sat up in his bed, gasping for air. It was dark so he switched on the bedside lamp and glanced around the room to make sure he was alone. He breathed a sigh of relief when he saw that no one else was in the room.

Earlier that evening, he had decided to go up to his room to get some sleep. The day had begun far too early and had been filled with too much excitement. He glanced at the alarm clock next to his bed. Although he had been asleep for only a couple of hours, he felt rested, as though he had slept the entire night.

Darren dragged himself to the head of the bed and leaned against the headboard. He stared at the wand on the nightstand for a few moments before picking it up. As he held the wand in his hand, he thought about his last dream. Was it a dream, or a vision of things to come? Nothing in the dream had looked familiar except for Marrion Lysbitt. His skin prickled when he thought about what Marrion had said to him in the dream. Darren knew that the few minutes he had shared with Marrion had to be a glimpse of the future. He thought about his family and Joe, and how they would all feel if they had to go through something like this again. *Maybe I'd be better off leaving them all behind.*

He sat deep in thought, his eyes lowered again to look at the wand in his hand, which was now glowing. Before long, the glow began to intensify and an image appeared in the crystal tip, illuminating his bedroom. Darren found himself sitting in his bed in the middle of a cobblestone street. People walked by him, through him and around him in a ghostly blue haze. A vendor, with her cart of small and fragile looking glass bottles full of mysterious liquids, was set up on the other side of the street in front of a few ancient little shops. None of the buildings looked familiar to him. This place was unfamiliar, like the one in his last dream. Just as quickly as it appeared, the scene disappeared.

"No, wait!" Darren cried out. "If that was the clue, I didn't get it. It was too fast. Oh, no." Darren's heart sank. He began to shake the wand. "Bring it back, please! I need more time," he begged.

The wand continued to glow. He held it in his hand and flicked it back and forth. After a few moments, the tip of the wand projected a word on the wall across the room. Darren scuttled to the foot of the bed to better position himself to read it. *Mixquic.*

"*Mixquic.* What does that mean? I don't understand? Is it a person? A place? A drink? Come on, what am I supposed to find? What is the artifact? Where is it? I need more!" Darren shouted.

The clue on the wall faded away and the wand's glow dimmed.

"Great!" Darren exclaimed. Frustrated, he flopped back down on his bed and stared at the ceiling.

He heard a soft knocking on his bedroom door. He sat up again, looking at the door. It slowly opened.

"Can I come in?" asked Sarah.

"Sure."

"I heard you talking and thought you might be having a bad dream." Sarah closed the door and crossed the floor to sit on the corner of the bed. She looked at the wand in Darren's hand.

"The wand sort of revealed the next clue," Darren informed her. "But I didn't understand what it was telling me," Darren said.

"What did it tell you?"

"It showed me a street with some people and shops, and then a word."

"What was the word?" she asked.

"Mixquic."

"Mixquic. That sounds familiar," Sarah replied. "Hold on, I'm going to get my laptop. I can look it up." Sarah exited the bedroom then returned with her laptop. Sitting on the edge of the bed she typed in Mixquic. "Is that how it was spelled?" she enquired.

"Yes," he answered, moving closer to the computer screen.

Seconds later, the page displayed a list of sites.

"Mixquic is a small town south-east of Mexico City," Sarah read out loud.

"Mexico City?" Darren asked.

"Yeah, apparently there's a spectacular celebration for Dia de Muertos, The Day of the Dead, every year. Hey, isn't the Carnival leaving for Mexico City?" Sarah asked.

"Yeah, it is," Darren answered softly.

"Well, you can't ignore the coincidence. You have to go."

"Yeah, I know. I mean, I'm supposed to, right?" Darren said, sounding confused. "I really don't know what to do. I want to go but I don't want to leave my family and friends. I will if I have to, though." He got up, walked to the window and gazed outside at the street. "I have to think about it."

"Well, don't stew over it too long. You have just half a day to figure it out," Sarah reminded him as she walked to the door. "Talk to you in the morning," she added before closing the bedroom door behind her.

Darren had decided it was better not to tell Sarah about his nightmare with Marrion. He didn't want her worrying or looking over her shoulder to see if she was being stalked by the crazed magician. Besides, Marrion, and whoever might be working with him, was after him and the artifact. He doubted very much that the magician would resort to his old tricks and come after the people Darren cared about. Darren believed that Lysbitt was angry enough to come after *him* next time.

Perhaps it wasn't a good idea to remain at home with a father who didn't trust him and jeopardize the safety of his friends and sister. Being around people with his same abilities who could teach him more about his unique talents, how to fit in and be accepted, how to do magic in front of crowds that would applaud and love his special gifts... now that might be worthwhile. Perhaps this town was not the right place for him. Maybe his destiny was to join the magicians and travel with them and the Carnival. By doing so, Darren believed he could protect his family and friends. In his heart, he knew it was the right thing to do. He knew his parents wouldn't let him go if he asked them and explaining to them why he had to go wouldn't be easy.

Chapter Sixteen

-Destination: Destiny-

Darren crawled back into bed but had a difficult time falling asleep; he couldn't turn off the thoughts in his mind. He knew he would have to get up an hour or so before his parents, awaken Sarah and then sneak out of the house without waking their parents or alerting the two officers parked out front.

When the time was right, Darren got out of bed and put on some clothes. He crept down the hallway to Sarah's bedroom and quietly opened her bedroom door. She was still asleep and snoring lightly. Darren leaned forward and gently squeezed her shoulder. Sarah awoke with a jerk and pushed Darren away as she scrambled to sit up.

"It's okay. It's just me," Darren whispered.

"What's wrong?" Sarah asked him, slightly agitated.

"I have to get to the Carnival and won't be able to once Mom and Dad are up. Dad wants to drag me off and use me as a guinea pig again today. The two officers out front can't see us leave or they'll follow us. Will you come with me?"

"Sure I'll go, but I don't agree with you about the officers. They should see us leave so they can follow us and assure Mom and Dad we weren't kidnapped," Sarah argued.

"I hadn't thought of that. Not bad, sis. You're a pro at this. They'll suspect something when I'm not with you later, though," Darren said, furrowing his brow.

"You've decided to go?"

Ignoring the question, Darren instructed her to get dressed and meet him at his bedroom. Once back in his room, he grabbed his backpack and proceeded to stuff clothes, toothbrush, hairbrush, toiletries and the wand into it. Sarah stood in the hallway where Darren could see her through the open bedroom door. After taking one final glance around his room, he swung his backpack over his shoulder, walked out into the hallway and closed his bedroom door. They exited the house by way of the front door. Darren waved at the police officers and proceeded to walk up the sidewalk in the direction of Joe's house.

"Aren't you going to take the car?" Sarah enquired.

"It would be too easy for them to follow us in a car."

"Right," Sarah responded.

When they reached Joe's house, they crept around to the backyard and tapped on his bedroom window. When no one responded, Darren peeked through the open window. Realizing that Joe wasn't awake, he reached in, picked up a baseball glove resting on the windowsill and hurled it across the room. The glove landed with a thud on the pillow next to Joe's head.

Joe leaped out of bed with one fist raised in the air and hollered, "I know I may only have one arm to fight you with, but be warned that I can still lay a pretty good beating!"

"Joe, it's Sarah and me," Darren said, chuckling.

Joe blinked a few times and glared at Darren "D, one of these days, man, my reflexes may actually be quicker than you think and you could end up with a black eye." He lowered his fist and took a few deep breaths.

"Sure, or you could have beaten that baseball glove black and blue," Darren smirked, pointing to the glove on Joe's pillow.

"You threw a glove at me? *Nice*," Joe said, nodding his head.

"Well, with your Jedi intuition, I didn't want a black eye," Darren quipped.

"Hey, you know it!" Joe replied, pulling a shirt over his head. "So, what's going on?"

"I have to get to the Carnival. They're leaving town today at noon. Thought you two might want to come with me to say goodbye."

At that moment Sarah glanced in the window and motioned for them to hurry up and get outside.

"They're your pals, not mine," Joe remarked. "Why would I want to say goodbye? That Vanrick guy is strange."

"He's like me, Joe—"

"He's got *abilities* like you, but he's not *like* you. D," Joe interjected.

"He's alright. He's teaching me things. He's showing me what I've become and what I'm capable of doing"

"Sure, I know he is," Joe said as they climbed out the window. "And I know I can't help you with that. I just think it's weird that he's so eager to hang out with you, that's all."

"Don't worry, Joe. He's a good guy," Darren assured him.

"If you say so," Joe replied with a shrug.

"Do I detect a little jealousy?" Sarah said, throwing her arm around Joe's shoulders.

"Not a chance," Joe said defensively.

Darren had turned away from Sarah and Joe and was looking back at the fence they had just passed. "Okay, guys, it's time to ditch the police escort. We have to sneak away without their knowledge; they have to believe we're still hanging out here with Joe." He crouched down low and crawled behind the hedge where he eyed the patrol car across the street.

When it was safe, the three of them sneaked to the backyard, which was surrounded by tall trees and a high wooden fence. Joe quickly walked over to his father's tool shed and grabbed an old wooden ladder.

"Good thinking, Joe!" Darren said enthusiastically. "That'll make it much easier."

Sarah was skeptical. "That's great for getting up, but how about climbing down the other side?"

"Well, our neighbors, the Andreasons, have their winter wood stock bin right next to the fence. That's the most logical place to climb," Joe informed her.

"Oh, I see. We can use the wood bin as a step. That's good thinking, Joe!" Sarah smiled at him encouragingly.

After Joe positioned the ladder against the fence, Darren suggested that Joe go over first so he could help Sarah down, if needed. Joe climbed up the ladder and swung his leg over the top of the fence. He looked down to see where to place his foot.

"Uh, guys, the Andreasons haven't cut their fire wood yet," Joe declared sheepishly.

Sarah groaned. Darren looked down at the ground, shaking his head.

"Good news, though!" Joe added happily. "The wood bin is still here. We just have to step onto the side of the bin and climb down. It's a bit of a stretch, so make sure you feel for the edge before you step down. I wouldn't jump if I were you 'cause I've done that before and broken my ankle. That wasn't fun at all."

"Go ahead, Sarah," Darren urged.

Sarah climbed up the ladder. "I really hate heights," she said as she swung her leg over the fence and stretched out her leg as far as she could to feel for the wooden bin. She felt someone touch her foot.

"I'll guide you," Joe said, as he moved her foot in the right direction. "You have to swing your other leg over or you won't reach it."

Supporting her weight with her hands and arms, Sarah carefully swung her other leg over. When she felt the rim of the bin, she pressed her toes down on it.

"Okay, you can let go now," Joe announced as Darren peered at them over the top of the fence.

Sarah hopped down off the bin. Before Darren swung his legs over the fence, he gave the ladder a gentle push. It fell down at the foot of the fence and was concealed in the tall grass. He climbed down the other side and smiled at the others. "A little adventure first thing in the morning never hurt anyone," he said, smiling.

"Oh, really? That's not what I hear," Sarah teased, winking at Joe.

Joe shyly averted her gaze. They crossed the neighbor's yard and paused in front of Joe's house.

"It will be a long walk to the Carnival, you know," Joe said.

"We can take a taxi from the coffee shop down the road."

"Mmm, coffee," Joe replied, closing his eyes.

"Yeah, I wouldn't mind a bagel, too," Sarah added.

"Mmm, bagel," Joe repeated, starting to drool.

"Well, let's pick up the pace then," Darren insisted, quickening his step.

The others hurried to keep up. The sun had risen but the temperature hadn't soared yet. As they walked past all the familiar houses, Darren recalled fond memories of his previous summers when he helped Mr. Davis cut his lawn and assisted Mrs. Matheson with odd jobs and yard work. He liked the old widow and would miss visiting her. As he gazed around him, he realized how much he would miss his neighborhood and his town.

When they reached the coffee shop, Darren, suggested they sit down for a little while. Darren went to the counter to order and then sat down with Joe and Sarah while the barista was preparing their coffees.

"Guys, I really need to tell you something," Darren said finally, setting his backpack on an empty chair next to him.

"Sure, fire away," Joe said with a mouthful of bagel.

"Two grandé caramel lattes and one grandé toffee nut latte," the barista announced as she placed the coffees on the bar.

"I'll get them," Sarah volunteered, leaping from her chair to retrieve the drinks.

"So what's up?" Joe asked.

"Just wait for Sarah," Darren said.

When Sarah returned to the table, Darren told them what was on his mind. "I've made a decision. I've decided to leave town with the Carnival this afternoon. They're headed for Mexico City," he explained.

"I knew it!" Sarah announced proudly.

"You knew it? How come she knew and I didn't?" Joe said, looking at Darren with cream cheese hanging off his lower lip.

"I just guessed he would go. It's the logical choice. You had to do it," Sarah explained.

"I belong with them. I'll be accepted and admired if I go with them. If I stay here, I'll always have to deal with people's intolerance, including my own father's. I don't understand why he isn't budging on this. It's really out of character for him."

"Yeah, we're talking about the guy who is open-minded about everything and ultra trusting," Sarah piped in. "Remember the time he invited that couple into our home during dinner? Their car had broken down and they asked to use the phone. Dad invited them to stay for dinner until the tow truck arrived," Sarah said.

"Jeez, they could have been psycho or something," Joe said, taking a sip of his latte. "Oh, yuck, what is this? This isn't my coffee!" he sputtered, choking on the hot brew.

Without thinking, Darren raised his hand and with a flick of his wrist switched the coffee with his own without touching the cup in front of Joe.

"Toffee nut," Joe muttered. "Who drinks toffee nut?"

Two children, who were waiting for their mother to order strawberry lemonades, had observed Darren's act of trickery.

"Nice magic trick!" Sarah exclaimed.

Darren looked at the kids and smiled. "Just practicing for my show," he said, winking.

The children beamed back delighted smiles. Their mother brought their drinks and sat down next to them. Darren looked away but overheard the little girl say, "Mommy, he's a real magician. We saw a trick."

The mother stroked the little girl's hair and replied, "That's nice, sweetie."

Darren couldn't help but smile; he would be accepted as a magician. The looks on Sarah and Joe's faces only helped to seal the deal. He knew in his heart that he had made the right decision.

Darren handed Sarah the note he had written for his parents explaining why he had to go. "Make sure you give this to them after you're sure there's enough distance between here and the Carnival," Darren instructed.

"D, can I go, too?" Joe asked.

"You should stay and protect Sarah. I don't think you'll be in danger once I leave here, but I don't want to take any chances. Besides, you should finish school first," Darren added.

"What about you? What are you going to do about school? You only have one more year," Sarah reminded him.

"I'm sure I can enroll in a school wherever I end up. And there's always correspondence. Don't worry, I'll finish school," Darren said reassuringly as he gave Sarah a shove.

"And you'll keep in touch, right?"

"Of course. I'll always keep you updated."

"You'd better, 'cause I plan on joining you eventually," Joe said matter-of-factly.

"I sure hope so," Darren said with a smile. He looked at his watch. "Well, I think we've been here long enough. The Carnival will be leaving in a couple of hours, so we should go."

Darren hoisted his backpack over his shoulder and waved goodbye to the two children. They tossed their empty coffee cups into the garbage bin as they headed for the door. Before leaving the coffee shop, Darren and Joe waved goodbye to the cute cashier behind the counter.

"I'll miss seeing her," Darren said, referring to the cashier.

"Hey, don't worry. While you're gone, I'll ask her out. Then I'll get to see her all the time," Joe said with a snicker.

Darren butted Joe with his shoulder, knocking him off the sidewalk.

"Hey, you never made a move on her," Joe reminded him.

"Very true," Darren admitted.

Sarah went to the phone booth and dialed the cab company while Darren headed across the street to use the bank machine. He would need some money to keep him going for awhile.

The taxi dropped them off in front of the entrance to the Carnival. The once colorful site that had been teeming with activity now looked barren and deserted. Most of the rides had been disassembled for the Carnival's departure. It was almost time for them to vacate the lot. Carnies everywhere were packing up equipment.

Darren, Joe and Sarah made their way to the magician's tent. For a moment Darren's heart sank, as though he had already left. Then he saw Alexius, Vanrick Frulis and another magician he hadn't met walking towards them. Behind them was a large tour bus with *Magic Tour Bus* written on the side.

"Wow! They must make some decent cash to afford that hotel on wheels." Joe exclaimed.

"Darren, we are very pleased to see you," Vanrick said, putting his hand on Darren's shoulder. "Darren, this is Alexius. I believe you caught one of his magic acts. And this is Manuel, also a magician with our group."

"Pleased to meet you both. It makes sense that I go with you, Vanrick," Darren said with a smile. "Besides, I have a destiny to fulfill."

"Don't we all," Alexius said. He eyed the backpack Darren was carrying. "Is that all you're bringing?"

"Yeah, this is everything I need," Darren answered confidently.

"Light packer. I think we'll get along just fine," Alexius said warmly. "Well, if you'll excuse me, I'll run ahead and make sure everything is loaded and everyone is behaving. See you on board. Let's get going, Manuel." Alexius nodded at Joe and Sarah and then walked toward the bus.

"Now that you have arrived, it really is time to go," Vanrick said to Darren. He bowed and took a large step backwards to allow the three young people to say goodbye in private.

"Well, at least you'll be travelling in style," Joe said, stepping closer to Darren. "I mean, I was picturing an old, rickety panel van or a wooden wagon to haul you *special* people around in."

"The bus is pretty sweet, huh?" Darren said with a smile that spread across his face. He would never admit it to Joe but he'd feared he'd be travelling in an old wooden wagon, too.

"I'll say. So, this is it, huh? You're sure you wanna go?" Joe asked.

Sarah looked down at the ground and kicked a little pebble.

"Yeah, I really have to, Joe. Sarah, you know I'm going to miss you. Right, twerp?" he asked. She slowly looked up to meet his gaze. "Oh, come on now. Don't be sad. I'll always be your brother and we'll never really be far apart. You know how to reach me if you need me or if you just want to say hi. You've done it before," Darren said, pulling his sister to him and giving her a big hug.

"Oh, come on, guys. This sucks! You're making me all weepy," Joe whined.

Darren and Sarah looked at Joe and laughed. Sarah threw her arm around him and pulled him into the embrace.

"I'm really going to miss you guys," Darren said.

"I'm going to miss you," Sarah said tearfully.

Joe let go of them and stepped back.

Sarah pulled away and looked at her brother. "Goodbye, Darren."

"No, this isn't goodbye. This is until next time," Darren corrected. "Well, I should go. They're waiting for me."

"Do your Jedi mind trick thing if you need help or anything," Joe quipped. "Or just pick up the phone. I'm kinda jealous, you know. After all, you're about to start an exciting adventure without your sidekick."

Darren returned Joe's smile. He'd never let them know how much his heart was aching at the thought of leaving them behind. And yet, somewhere deep in another part of his heart, excitement and anticipation were stirring. "You two take care. Sarah, let Mom and Dad know this was the right thing for me. I'll see you guys later," Darren said finally before turning around. Vanrick joined him and they walked to the bus together.

"He's not even going to look back at us," Sarah said ruefully as she watched him walk away.

"He'd better not, or I'll cry," Joe said. Sarah turned and punched him in the arm.

"Ouch! That hurt!" he said, giving Sarah a playful shove.

"You're a baby," Sarah said jokingly.

When Darren and Vanrick reached the bus, Vanrick turned to him. "You're going to be a great magician, Darren. Have you considered a stage name in case anyone tries to find you? It wouldn't be a bad idea, you know. Over time, most magicians come up with a stage name. It doesn't have to be unusual. Some magicians just change their first or last name."

"I think I'll use the name Darius," Darren said.

"I thought you might," Vanrick said. "Don't worry about Joe and Sarah. They'll be just fine."

"I know they will. And I know this will be a very interesting journey," Darren said with a smile as he stepped onto the bus and was greeted by the smiling faces of the other magicians on board.

He never looked back. He was moving forward towards his destiny and a new and truly magical future.

Don't miss out on the adventure!

Coming summer 2007

APPEARANCE:
The Second Part of Trickery
and Honest Deception

Book Two of the Trickery and Honest Deception
Chronicles
by
Rachelle G. Adamchuk

ISBN 141208991-3